Praise for You Have Me to Love

'In this tremendous book, Robben explores isolation, guilt, mother- and childhood in the most unexpected way. Robben's crystal clear sentences combined with his deep gaze into the flipsides of human behavior – and love – make this an unforgettable read. Run to the bookstores, people'
DORTHE NORS

'An overwhelming debut about lost childhood innocence, *You Have Me to Love* can be favourably compared to Niccolò Ammaniti's *I'm Not Scared* and Ian McEwan's *The Cement Garden*. A staggering first novel: faultless in its description of a child's inner world'
Het Parool

'What a beautiful writer Robben is! I read the novel and was completely seduced – raw and harrowing and very moving. Robben is a powerful writer and reminds me very much of Per Petterson'
AIFRIC CAMPBELL

'This is a bold, tender and ambivalent narrative, raw and disturbing, with moments of painful beauty: a taut narrative heavy with a convincing sense of dread'
Irish Times

'Robben lifts you from your life and sweeps you away, with no chance of escaping. You just keep reading while you're holding your breath. A promising novelist is born'
De Morgen

'A gripping novel that steadily tightens its hold'
De Volkskrant

'*You Have Me to Love* is a beautiful, intoxicating book full of magnificent sentences and terrific empathy'
Boekblad

'Beautiful, just beautiful'
GERBRAND BAKKER

'Lucid and unjudgemental, this a universal story of isolation, loneliness and tragedy. Like a record stuck in its groove, it won't let me go'
EUROPEAN LITERATURE NETWORK

'A small masterpiece'
Harpers Bazaar

'Mixes the sinister with the beautiful to create something truly unique'
Blackwell's Book Shop

'From the very first sentence it is clear how well début novelist Jaap Robben writes. His childishly simple yet highly suggestive sentences make *You Have Me to Love* as stark and foreboding as the island on which it is set'
NRC Next

'Unbelievable. A beautiful story, light for all its heaviness, written in a clear and powerful style. Robben merges grief, simplicity and isolation in a phenomenal way'
Telegraaf

'Robben's clear sentences and empathic use of language read like poetry: rhythmic, probing, and sonorous'
Dagblad van het Noorden

'A beautiful novel about grief, remorse and loneliness, which excels in its level of sophistication'
Algemeen Dagblad

'Robben shows in a sober, visual, poetic style how mother and son keep each other prisoner, unable to live either with or without each other'
Nederlands Dagblad

'Robben is a wizard with the written word. On every page you come across sentences of no more than six or seven words that transform in your head into succinct, artful, razor-sharp films. *You Have Me to Love* is a true joy to read'
Boek

'Robben's prose is beautiful and expressive'
Hotel Boekenlust

'In restrained and austere language, it pierces your heart directly to its core'
ZiN Magazine

'Robben has just written himself straight into literary history'
Boekenredactie Bol.com

'Magnificent, poetic, lonely, gruesome. And also beautifully written'
Kunststof Radio 1

'You have those books that you can't put down, but that you also want to savour for as long as possible because other-wise they are over too soon. *You Have Me to Love* by Jaap Robben is one of those books'
Boekenbijlage.nl

JAAP ROBBEN (1984) is a poet, playwright, performer and acclaimed children's author. *You Have Me to Love*, his first novel for adults, has received international glowing reviews and is the winner of the 2014 Dutch Booksellers Award, the Dioraphte Prize, and the ANV Award for best Dutch debut. To date, the novel has sold over 50,000 copies in the Netherlands and is available in ten languages. *You Have Me to Love* is currently being adapted into an English-language film.

DAVID DOHERTY studied English and literary linguistics in Glasgow before moving to Amsterdam, where he has been working as a translator since 1996. His translations include novels by critically acclaimed Dutch-language authors: *The Dutch Maiden* by Marente de Moor (long-listed for the Warwick Translation Prize 2017), *Monte Carlo* by Peter Terrin, and *The Dyslexic Hearts Club* by Hanneke Hendrix. He has also translated the work of leading Dutch sports writers Hugo Borst and Wilfried de Jong. David was recently commended by the jury of the Vondel Translation Prize for his translations of *The Dutch Maiden* and *You Have Me to Love*.

You Have Me to Love

JAAP ROBBEN

You Have Me to Love

Translated from the Dutch by
David Doherty

WORLD EDITIONS
New York, London, Amsterdam

Published in the USA in 2018 by World Editions LLC, New York
Published in the UK in 2016 by World Editions LTD, London

World Editions
New York/London/Amsterdam

Printed by Sheridan, Chelsea, MI, USA

This book is a work of fiction. Any resemblance to actual persons,
living or dead, or actual events is purely coincidental.

Library of Congress Cataloging in Publication Data is available.

ISBN 978-1-64286-001-6

First published as *Birk* in the Netherlands in 2014 by De Geus BV.

This project has been funded with support from the European
Commission. This publication reflects the views only of the author,
and the Commission cannot be held responsible for any use which
may be made of the information contained herein.

This book was published with the support of
the Dutch Foundation for Literature

Twitter: @WorldEdBooks
Facebook: WorldEditionsInternationalPublishing
www.worldeditions.org

For Patrick

Many thanks to Ad, Sander, Thijs, Marieke, the World Editions and the De Geus family. To Passa Porta for providing me with a pleasant and quiet place to work at the right moment. To Henk for *hoppakee*, the word that hung above my computer and kept me going. To my loving parents, Sylvia and Gerard, for unfailing support and pots of soup. To David, for his loving translation. And thanks to my own sweet Suus, without whom this book would never have seen the light of day.

I

1

My tongue felt like it was crawling with ants. My feet were heavy. I was standing at the back door in my swimming trunks, towel around my neck. Mum had come into the kitchen, but she hadn't looked at me yet. 'There you are,' she said without raising her head as she lifted the lid off the pot. She ladled my bowl full of soup, then hers.

She dipped a finger into my soup and stirred. 'Just right. Tuck in.' I sat down on my chair and stared at the steam rising sluggishly from my bowl. 'Don't leave too much for Dad. If he'd wanted a decent helping, he should've been back on time.' Spooning soup into her mouth, she returned to her sewing machine in the living room. 'Just finishing this off. Won't be long.'

My hands lay motionless on the table. Inside they were shaking. I could hear the scraping of gulls sharpening their beaks on the gutter above the window. I knew I should be eating my soup, but it was all I could do to take hold of the spoon.

I took a gulp of water from my glass. It felt like I was choking. I gagged and a little of what I sicked up disappeared into my soup. I wiped away what had landed next to the bowl with a furtive sweep of my hand. Mum hadn't noticed. She was leaning forward in her chair, staring intently at the rattling needle of her sewing machine, only letting up to see if she was still going in a straight line.

After a few minutes, Mum came back into the kitchen to fetch the Worcester sauce from the spice rack. She rested her hips against the sink and leaned toward the window.
'Taking his own sweet time again.' My heart wanted to leap out of my chest. I stuck the empty spoon in my mouth. 'Don't take after your father,' she smiled. 'You can never count on a man like that.' Before I could answer, the sewing machine had started rattling again.

The harder I bit down on my tongue, the more the ants prickled. Dusk made a mirror of the window. I knew it held my reflection, but I couldn't bring myself to look. Mum went over to the bin, trod on the pedal, and let a few scraps of material fall from her hand.
'Aren't you going to eat anything?'
I gave a jerky shrug.
'Nothing to say for yourself?'
'I've had enough,' I said.
'Well, that wasn't much.'
'Sorry.'
'Don't come crying like a baby that you want something else later.' She tipped my soup back into the pot, placed my bowl next to hers by the sink, and left the pot and one bowl on the table for Dad. She caught me looking at them. 'That father of yours can heat up his own soup.' When she called him 'that father of yours', it meant he'd done something he needed to make up for. She rubbed dark-brown stripes across the table with a damp cloth.

'He swam away.' The words stumbled out of my mouth.

'Hmm?'

'Dad swam away.'

'"Swam away"?'

'Yes.'

'How do you mean?'

'Dunno.'

She looked at me, puzzled. 'Where to?'

I shrugged.

'Didn't he tell you?'

Again, I shrugged.

'But you must know if he said something.'

'I don't think he said anything.'

She cupped her hands around her eyes and put her face to the window.

'Did you two have a row?'

'No.'

She tossed her head as if to shake loose a couple of strange thoughts.

'That waster does whatever he likes.' She turned the tap on full, put the plug in the sink, and squirted in some washing-up liquid. I heard the muffled clunk of plates and mugs, the scrape of knives, forks, and spoons. The boiler hummed away in the cupboard below.

At the slightest sound, Mum looked up and turned her head toward the front door, though they were only the noises the house makes. When she was finished, she draped a tea towel over the clean dishes on the draining board.

'He was underwater.'

'What?'

'All of a sudden.'

'What was all of a sudden?'

I shrugged.

'Stop shrugging your shoulders every time I ask you a question.'

'He wanted to climb out of the water after me.'

'Did you two go swimming?'

'No.'

'You *knew* that wasn't allowed.'

I shook my head.

'What happened? Tell me.'

'I looked round and all of a sudden Dad was swimming underwater.'

'Underwater? Just like that?'

I tried my best not to shrug, but I couldn't help myself.

'He must have said something?'

'Dunno.'

'Well, where did he go?'

'I don't know that, either.'

'Dunno, dunno, dunno... Where was he heading?'

'I couldn't see.'

'But you just said he climbed out of the water after you.'

'Didn't.'

'What do you mean, "didn't"?'

'I didn't go for a swim.'

Her hand shot out and felt at my swimming trunks. 'Are you telling me lies?'

My head wouldn't stop shaking.

'Where were you?'

'On the sand.'

'And that's where he went swimming?'

I shook my head. 'Over by the rocks.'

She looked deep into my eyes. Then she rushed into the hall, yanked open the dresser drawer, and took out a torch. She flashed it on and off three times and went outside. By the time the light on the outside wall flickered on, she had disappeared round the side of the house. Quick as I could, I pulled one of Dad's jumpers from the drying rack and put it on. It was way too big for me. I wormed my feet into my boots and had to run to keep up with her.

2

The red light of a buoy appeared in the distant dusk. We scrambled down the path to the beach, curled like a half-moon around the cove. I kept trying to take hold of Mum's hand, but she was walking too fast.

Dad's sunglasses, his towel, and our flip-flops lay waiting on the sand, but not where we'd left them. I felt a surge of relief. Dad must have climbed out of the water and moved our things further from the breaking waves. Seconds later, my legs turned weak and wobbly again as I realized the tide had gone out.

Mum shoved the torch into my hands and turned over the things on the sand, as if he might be hiding under them. 'Birk!' she shouted across the water. 'Where are you?'

When no answer came, she turned to me. I accidentally shone the light in her face.

'Where did you see him last?'

I pointed the torch at the rocks.

'There?'

I was close to tears.

'Are you sure?' She didn't see me nod. She was staring out to sea again. 'Birk!' she shouted. 'Birk!'

Unbroken silence. Not even the gulls were squawking.

As soon as Mum started walking, I followed her with the torch so she could see where she was putting her feet. Without hesitation, her shoes walked into the sea. The water was soon up to her knees. She seemed to be in shock as she took in all that dark water tugging at her shoes, growing wider with every step.

I tried to shine the torch in the direction she was looking. Any second now, Dad would surface, coughing and choking, and here she was, ready to grab hold of him and haul him up onto the beach. Any second now, he would emerge from the water. He had to. Especially now that Mum was here. We'd see his head above the waves, like a football floating toward us. 'Look! Look over there,' I'd shout, jumping onto Mum's back and catching him in the torchlight. We'd wade further into the sea, put his arms around our shoulders the way they do in films, and help him ashore. After that he'd probably belt me one across the face, but I wouldn't care. At least he'd be back.

'Tell me.' Mum gripped my chin between her thumb and forefinger. 'Tell me what happened here.'

'He was swimming, I think. That's what it looked like. And all of a sudden he was underwater and further and further away.'

'And what did you do?'

I fell silent.

'Why didn't you tell me right away?'

'But I did tell you.'

She snatched the torch from my hands and we rounded the cove till we reached the rocks. We balanced on the boulders and tore open our hands on the barnacles. Normally she'd be nagging me to be careful up here, but now she kept climbing on ahead and calling out his name.

Suddenly I caught sight of something in a small inlet. A dark object was floating in the water a few feet below me, thumping and splashing. I wanted to jump in, but I wasn't brave enough. I shouted to Mum a few yards up ahead. 'I've found something!'

She slipped and dropped the torch. It rolled away but came to rest in a crevice between two rocks. She scrambled to her feet, picked up the torch, and lunged toward me. 'Where? Where?' Anxiously, she aimed the torch at the dark water beneath us. A tree trunk covered in seaweed was slamming into the rocks. 'Oh Christ,' she shouted. 'Jesus fucking Christ.'

We clambered on. At the highest point she stopped and sent a beam of light skimming across the water. Her shouting had turned to pleading. I yelled out, 'Dad-dad-daaaaad!'

Half walking, half running, we headed back home, torchlight bouncing over the path. I wanted to say something to help us catch our breath. Maybe Dad was already home. Maybe he'd taken another path. We'd probably just missed him along the way. Or maybe he'd swum right round the island, and now he was sitting at the kitchen table, wolfing down a bowl of soup.

The silence hit us in the face. Everything in the kitchen was just as we'd left it. The big pot of soup, his bowl, the spoon beside it. I almost forgot to breathe.

Mum moved like a restless animal that's sensed a change in the weather. 'Karl,' she said. 'I have to get Karl.' The door handle rammed into the wall. Grains of plaster crumbled to the floor. I went to follow her, but she jabbed a pointed finger toward the kitchen. 'Stay here, you.'

3

Now that I was alone, the cupboards around me seemed to grow taller. The bright kitchen light left dark specks floating in my eyes. I couldn't bring myself to look at anything, didn't dare sit down. It felt like I was being stared at from all sides. I switched off the big light and then the light in the hood above the cooker. I waited till my eyes got used to the dark, and crept upstairs.

Still wearing my boots, swimming trunks, and Dad's jumper, I hid under the blanket. My breathing was ragged. When I closed my eyes, a pale shape appeared. I could see gulls circling around me, terns sitting on the rocks or diving for fish, and all the while that same pale shape. I switched on the bedside lamp, but that only scared me more, crushing any doubt that I might not be awake. I turned the lamp off and the shape returned. Other things, too: the towel that seemed further from the sea, a hand that would not break the surface. The pale shape blurred, grew vaguer. I pressed my fingers against my eyes till all I could see were flashes of light.

It was like I'd accidentally held a burning candle too close to the curtains, and there was no putting out the fire. Like I'd dropped something and it had shattered, something I wasn't allowed to touch. I wanted a hand to slap me hard enough and long enough to start up that constant whistling in my ear. Once I'd been punished, it would all be okay again. Done and dusted.

Somewhere outside I could hear the engine of Karl's cutter starting up. Pressing my ear to the mattress, the drone became clearer, as if someone was scratching at the underside of my bed.

Karl would turn on the big searchlight on top of his

cabin and point it at the beach and the rocky inlets. From the water he would scan all the places we had searched, in the hope that we'd missed something. He'd sail further from the beach, past the rocks where it's too dangerous to swim, and then further out. Perhaps he'd sail right round the island and then go round again, just in case, sailing in ever increasing circles till the waves grew too wild and the sea too big. Then he'd turn the wheel, look at Mum and shake his head.

No, no, no. They would find Dad. He would wave to them. He'd have found my red ball, he'd been able to hang on to it all along. And Dad wouldn't need any help from anyone. He'd climb aboard all by himself.

4

A mosquito was whining its way into my ear. I woke with a start and crushed it. Turning on the bedside lamp, I saw wings, blood, and legs stuck to my finger.

Light was coming from downstairs, hurried footsteps across the floor, talk from the kitchen. The net around my chest tightened again. I leapt out of bed and ran downstairs.

Mum was standing at the sink with her back to me, the hair on her neck spiky with sweat. She was on the phone. Catching sight of me in the doorway behind her, she jumped but kept on talking.

The coastguard, harbours, ferry companies, the fish-processing plant, she called them all. It was the same conversation every time. Birk Hammermann was missing. At sea. No, further west. West of Tramsund. Early that evening, a few hours ago. Swimming. In which direction? No, no idea. Looked everywhere. No, it's a small island, no other place he could be. Impossible to get lost, that's how small it is. Wait? No, why? He must be at sea. The water's cold. Search now before it's too late. She spelled his name. 'B-I-R-K, and Hammermann with two Ns.' As if that would help them recognize him at sea. Then Mum gave our telephone number and begged them to call the moment there was any news. Without saying goodbye, she'd break the connection and start punching in a new number.

I was still standing by the door. She pressed her bony hands against my cheeks, trying to squeeze an answer from my mouth. 'Where is Birk? Where is he?' All I could do was cry.

'Tell me.' She forced her fists harder into my face. 'Stop your blubbering. Tell me where Dad is.'

We went out searching, again and again. Each time I had to point out where we'd been sitting, and exactly where he'd gone into the water. The light from the torch grew dimmer. Mum shouted to Karl out in his boat, but he couldn't hear her over the din of his engine. He kept on sailing in circles, churning up the water. A gull squawked from time to time. Back in the kitchen, the phone calls began again.

Gradually everything around us began to glow dark blue. Morning came unnoticed.

5

A helicopter flew over. Our whole house rattled. Trees thrashed around, shedding yellow leaves. Plastic garden chairs tumbled and flew into the hedge. The helicopter circled above the island and then swooped low across the waves, whipping up the surface of the water as if to expose what was underneath.

After a while, it flew back in our direction and hung for a short while above the grassy slope behind the house. It tried to land but didn't seem able to. I could see two men behind the glass. They both raised a hand and flew off toward the horizon.

Later the coastguard called to say they had found nothing, and that the slope on our island was too steep for the helicopter. They needed to know the exact time of the disappearance to locate Dad in the current that had taken him out to sea. Mum looked at me.

'What time did you last see Dad?'

'I don't know,' I whispered, and began to cry again. 'It was still light.'

'Late afternoon, perhaps as late as six,' she answered.

The coastguard said they would keep a lookout, and that all shipping had been notified.

Mum kept on phoning. Her eyes were red and puffy, as if they'd been stung. She repeated her story. The answer was always the same: 'We'll do what we can.' Then she headed back outside, wearing Dad's raincoat. I had to wait by the phone. As soon as she was gone, I retreated into the darkness of the cupboard under the stairs. When the telephone shattered the silence, I let it ring till it stopped all by itself.

Even in my hiding place, the pale shape reappeared. I

pressed my fingers into my eyes till the pain made me cry out.

6

Karl knocked on the back door. Mum waved at me to open it.

Solemnly he took off his cap and shook my hand. The air around him was thick and tepid, his cheeks were bristly. He glanced around the kitchen and shrugged. 'Nothing,' he said, with a shake of his head. 'Not a trace.'

We all looked in different directions.

'They sometimes surface after three days or so,' Karl said.

I saw Dad rising from the deep, the arc of a diver in reverse: world underwater swimming champion Birk Hammermann. We'd all applaud, and Mum would stick her fingers in her mouth and whistle, and I'd give it a go, too. They'd let me keep the fake gold medal, and everything would turn out all right.

'Yeah,' he continued. 'And if they wash up on shore, they're all swollen up like that dead seal a while back.'

Mum leaned stiffly against the sink. I tried to imagine how long a person could hold their breath.

'There's no knowing where, eh. Could be anywhere. Pull of the water. Currents are treacherous, he should've ...' He let the rest of his words evaporate. 'He was... I mean is... a grown man.'

To prove how thoroughly he'd searched, he listed everything his nets had dredged up. 'Planks, old nets, seaweed. A plastic crate I lost months ago,' he chuckled. Flies were orbiting the kitchen light, spinning faster and faster, closing in on one another with a high-pitched buzz. There was no counting them.

Heaving a sigh, Karl looked at the pot of soup, still standing on the table since yesterday evening, along with the spoon and the empty bowl. The grey chunks of fish and broken strands of vermicelli had sunk to the bottom and fat glistened on the top. Karl scratched his head, stuck his little finger in his ear, and poked it around. He examined what his nail had scraped out and wiped it off on his trousers. 'Can't say I know what to do now,' he murmured.

Mum had turned to face the window. She wanted Karl to leave, to go on searching, to turn the sea inside out. He didn't get the message.

'Nothing else left to do,' he went on. 'You saw the helicopter.'

Karl took hold of Dad's chair, scraped it toward him, and sat down. The wickerwork seat creaked. He lowered his head. The flies had landed and were scuttling across the table. Nothing else in the kitchen moved.

Karl nodded toward the pot of soup. When I didn't respond, he turned to Mum. His neck was covered in blond hair that disappeared beneath the grubby collar of his shirt. Mum used to cut his hair once in a while. He would sit there, bare-chested, on one of the kitchen chairs, his head bent forward as Mum ran the trimmer over his neck. He had one of those belly buttons that stick out a bit. Dad always went outside to chop wood when Karl dropped by for a haircut. After he'd swept up and Mum had tucked the trimmer back in the toilet bag, Karl would hang around the kitchen much longer than he needed to, shirtless.

Karl had pulled the soup bowl toward him. He eyed the spoon, turned it over between his fingers, and tapped it lightly on the table. 'What can I do?' he said. 'I suppose I could let down my nets and sail round the island again.' Mum didn't answer.

I began to count. I'd nearly reached a hundred before Karl said, 'Just don't know what else to do.' He stood up and said goodbye. Mum's lips creased into a thin line.

The chug of Karl's boat brought her back to life. She lifted the pot from the table and sloshed the soup down the toilet. She took a brick of soup out of the freezer, clattered it into the empty pot, and turned the gas on full. The block of ice steamed and shrank while she stared out the window.

'We have to keep our strength up,' she said. She ladled Dad's bowl full and pushed it toward me. I'd rather have had a fresh one. 'Even if you're not hungry, you should try and eat something.'

'You too,' I said softly.

'I can't right now, love.' Every word sounded like a gasp, as if she were forcing them out with the last of her breath.

'What if I make *you* some soup?' I asked.

Her gaze turned tender as a kiss.

'You eat for both of us. Please. When Dad comes back, we'll eat together again.'

Silently, I began to spoon. A few mouthfuls were all I could manage.

Without a word, Mum went into the hall, wriggled her feet into her boots, and disappeared outside.

As soon as I could no longer hear her, I went to the toilet and poured the rest of my soup away. I rinsed the soup bowl and the spoon under the tap, dried them, and put them back on the table, where they had spent one whole day waiting for Dad.

7

We drank our coffee, awkward, silent. I had never seen Mum smoke, yet here she was, lighting Dad's cigarettes. She sucked fire into them expectantly, but after a couple of draws she let the fag end drop, hissing, into the last of her coffee. Stretching her arm, she slipped the pack back into the inside pocket of Dad's raincoat, which was slung over his chair.

It wasn't long before she fished the pack out again, and her trembling fingers slid a new cigarette between her lips. She saw me looking at her, and they curled into a smile as fragile as a Christmas-tree decoration, the kind you're afraid might break before you even touch it.

I dashed upstairs to my room, took the atlas from my desk, sat down on the bed, and opened it on my lap. I flicked through the pages, so fast I accidentally tore one. At the back there were maps of the sea, covered in wavy lines with arrows at the end. I was looking for the map with our stretch of sea. Our island wasn't on the map, but I knew where it was cos Dad had marked the spot with a little cross.

It was Dad who had taught me how to read the map, standing in the grass behind our house with the open atlas. From the top of the slope, we could see for miles.

'Well? Where are they?' I asked.

'Currents aren't something you can see, but they're everywhere.'

'Like God, you mean?'

He laughed. 'That's different.'

'Different how?'

'God is made up.'

'And currents aren't?'

'No.' He spread out his arms. 'They're everywhere.'

'So how do you know they're real?'

'You can feel them.'

I nodded. I thought I understood. 'If you can feel something, then it's real.'

'Something like that. Yes.'

I found the page with the little cross in the sea and traced my finger along the dark-blue lines in the water. Then I leafed through the other maps. The currents travelled halfway across the world, heading north, then arching right across the ocean to North America, down past Brazil, all the way down to Antarctica, and back. Eventually the currents came out not far from where they started. They came back to us.

That's how Dad would come back, and when the time came, I had to be the first to spot him. I climbed up on my desk and took the binoculars down off the top shelf.

It was a clear day. My gaze flashed back and forth over the waves and I tried to adjust the focus. Something black shot up from beneath the surface and I dropped the binoculars in fright. It was only a stupid shag.

My eyes jumped and jerked across the endless grey. I sighted a sailing boat on the horizon. With the naked eye, the sail was as small as a folded piece of paper, but through the binoculars I could see someone standing under the boom in a red coat. Up front there was someone else in a blue coat. I fiddled with the focus and saw it was the jib in its plastic cover.

All at once I lost sight of the boat, and it took a while for me to find it again. I knew that mustn't happen when Dad reappeared. When I shouted to Mum to come and see, I mustn't accidentally move the binoculars and lose sight of him, so I practised on rocks, gulls, and a bit of floating timber. I lowered the binoculars and then tried to relocate what I'd been looking at as quickly as possible. To make it more real, I tried shouting. I was getting better and better at it, though the gulls were tricky cos they moved so fast and I could never really tell if I'd found the right one again.

The door swung open. Mum stood there, staring at me wide-eyed. She was wearing Dad's nightshirt. I could see a bushy triangle of hair below it.

'What's the matter?' I asked.

'What's the matter with you?' she replied, breathless.

'Nothing.'

'Did you see something?'

'No.'

'But you were shouting.'

'Wasn't.'

'But I heard you.'

'I'm practising.'

'For what?'

'For when Dad comes back.'

She grabbed the binoculars, which were hanging from a cord around my neck, peered out to sea in no particular direction, and then let them fall. They slammed hard against my chest. It hurt, but I didn't let on.

8

A blue boat came motoring toward us, POLICE in big letters on the bow. It had a steel arc at the back with aerials sticking out, a kind of lunchbox on a pole, and two blue lights that weren't flashing. A searchlight was mounted on the roof of the cabin. Gulls came swooping in, thinking there was grub to be had. I chucked my binoculars on the bed, thundered down the stairs, and ran outside without my coat on.

The boat was already turning alongside the quay. The tyres on the bow scraped and groaned against the concrete. The engine sputtered. A boyish man in a baseball cap stood up front. You could tell right off he wasn't important cos they only let him hold the rope. Another man came out of the cabin and held up his hand to me. He ducked back inside and came out again wearing a policeman's cap. He was much more important, I reckoned. A third policeman stayed behind in the cabin.

'Why didn't you have the siren and the flashing lights on?'

The policeman with the cap smiled.

'Because there's no need.'

They let me take the rope and wrap it around the mooring post. I tied three different knots so they could see they weren't just dealing with some dopey little kid.

'That's tight enough. We're going to have to untie them in a bit.' The policeman with the cap stepped over the rail and jumped onto the quay. 'The Hammermanns?'

'I'm the son.'

'Sorry about your father.'

'He's called Birk,' I said. 'And Hammermann is with two Ns.'

'Yep, that's what we have here.' He held up some papers that were stapled together.

'Admundsen.' He held out his hand to me. 'You can call me Johan. I work for the police in Tramsund.'

'I'm Mikael.'

Johan was tall and had nicks on his throat from shaving. 'Clean cut,' Mum would call it. A couple of dark hairs were sticking out of his nose. 'So, here we are,' he said as he looked around. 'I've seen bigger places.'

'Two houses.'

'No one else?'

'There's a house over on the other side of the island, but it's been empty for a few years. It used to be Miss Augusta's.'

Smoke curled hesitantly from Karl's chimney. He had closed the curtains in his kitchen and living room.

'Who lives there?'

'Our neighbour,' I said.

'So that must be your house,' he said, pointing to ours.

'Uh-huh.'

'Does your neighbour have a name?'

'Karl.'

'Karl what?'

'Just Karl.'

'And is this Karl at home?'

'Do you want to talk to him?'

'Maybe in a little while.'

I looked at his papers. 'Shouldn't you be writing stuff down?'

'Like what?'

He saw me look startled. 'Writing stuff down comes later. I can remember everything for now. First things first: can you take me to see your mother?'

'What about those two?'

'They'll be all right where they are.' The man from the cabin was leaning against the bow and pouring coffee from a thermos flask into a plastic cup. The boy who was only allowed to hold the rope was strolling across the quay, kicking stones as if they were in his way.

'Before we go back, would you like to take a little trip with us?'

'Maybe,' I said, though I really, really wanted to.

Mum came running toward us, her eyebrows two desperate little arcs. 'Is there any news?'

Johan shook his head. ''Fraid not. I'm sorry about your husband.' He held out his hand. 'Admundsen. I'm in charge of the investigation. I've come to take care of the formalities for the missing-at-sea report, and I have a few questions to ask you.'

Without looking at him, Mum gave Johan a limp handshake and trudged back to the house. I followed behind her with Johan. I felt a sudden urge to hold his hand but luckily I stopped myself just in time. He saw me looking up at him and gave me a friendly nod.

'Am I interrupting your meal?' Johan pointed at the soup bowl.

'That's for Dad,' I said.

'Naturally.'

I didn't understand what he meant, so I said, 'Yes, naturally.'

Dad had taught me that you're supposed to offer visitors something to drink, but nothing too nice or you might never get rid of them. 'Can I get you anything?'

'That's nice of you.'

'There's some coffee left,' said Mum.

'Coffee would be just the ticket.'

'What do you take?'

'Sugar.'

I nodded and walked over to the sink.

'I can drink it without, too.'

'You want sugar, you'll get sugar,' said Mum.

It was only when we had visitors from somewhere else that I noticed how different our words sounded. Outsiders spoke more forcefully, and their voices took a funny turn at the end of their sentences. Mum could talk like that, too. 'Town talk' Dad called it, and always gave her a kiss as soon as he'd said it cos he knew she didn't like it. 'I didn't learn much from my mother, but at least she taught me to speak properly,' she'd say, pushing Dad away, though she'd end up letting him kiss her neck anyway.

Johan sighed. 'So... no news for the time being, it pains me to say.'

Mum stared straight at him.

'It's been forty-eight hours. The sea is a big place, Mrs Hammermann. But we're doing our best. Everyone is hoping for a miracle or suchlike.'

'Suchlike?'

'The strangest things happen. You'd be surprised.'

'What do you mean by that?'

'Sometimes people turn up out of nowhere. Things aren't always what they seem.'

'My son was there when it happened.' She pointed at the sea. 'That's where my husband is.' She'd slipped from her town accent back into her normal way of talking.

I put a mug of coffee on the table and fetched the sugar bowl from the cupboard. Johan flickered a faint smile at me and unfolded his papers.

'Let's hope for a miracle.' He took a sip of coffee, even though it was still far too hot and he hadn't put any sugar in it. 'Right, then, we'll start with the details.' Like the man on the news, he began to read out what was on the paper. 'Birk Hammermann, born 22 April 1963. Married to Dora Hammermann. That's you.' He nodded at Mum. 'Missing since the evening before last. Your report came in at forty-six minutes past eight. The coastguard was notified at twelve minutes past nine, after which time the standard procedure for "person missing at sea" was initiated. Yesterday morning a fellow officer attempted to make a landing on the island in the coastguard helicopter but unfortunately this did not prove possible. Okay... And then we have your witness statement.'

Mum breathed heavily through her nose.

'To enable us to obtain a full picture, could you tell me once again exactly what happened?'

'You already know what happened.'

'Please, tell us again,' he said. 'So we have the full picture. It's standard procedure in cases like this.'

Mum snatched the papers from his hand and clutched them to her chest. 'You're giving up your search?'

'May I have my forms back?'

'What exactly are you *doing*?'

'Everything in our power, Mrs Hammermann.'

'And that is?'

'Shipping has been notified. The coastguard has been conducting a search with two boats and a helicopter and a heat sensor. But due to the currents...'

Mum kicked the table leg, sending coffee spilling over the brim of the mug. 'I insist you keep on searching.'

Johan got up, walked over to Mum, and carefully removed the crumpled papers from her hands. For a moment no one made a sound. 'Your son is the last person to have seen him?' Mum crossed her arms and held them high against her chest. Johan turned to me.

'You were there with your father. What happened? Can you tell me?'

'Maybe.'

He looked back at Mum. 'May I speak to your son alone for a moment?'

'I'd rather you didn't.'

'Why not?'

'I should be here with him.'

'He'll be all right on his own for a minute or two. Why don't you step into the hall and I'll call you when you're needed.'

Mum didn't budge.

'Please, Mrs Hammermann. We want to find your husband as much as you do.'

She left the room but stood in the hall listening. I could see her face, distorted by the pebbled glass window in the door.

'Sorry about Mum,' I whispered.

'It's completely understandable. She's upset. It's no small matter, losing your husband.'

'Dad isn't lost.'

He bent down toward me. I caught the glint of a gold chain between two buttons of his shirt.

'You don't think so?'

I stared at the tabletop. 'No.'

'Well,' Johan continued. 'Tell me. How old are you?'

'Nine.'

He nodded as if I'd said something very important.

'Shouldn't you be at school?'

'Dad teaches me everything.'

'Everything?'

'Yes, we've got schoolbooks for arithmetic, English, geography, all sorts. A couple of hours a day. They send me tests every three months. Do you want to see them?'

I was giving him my very best attempt at town talk.

'In a little while, perhaps. First we need to talk about what happened the day before yesterday. Do you remember what time it was?'

I was a bit shaken to find that we were talking about Dad again. 'It was almost evening, I think.'

'And you were there when he drowned.'

'You're not allowed to say that,' I hissed.

'So what did happen?'

'He was swimming underwater for a while. All of a sudden.'

'For a while? And then he came back up again?'

I shrugged my shoulders.

'Did he come up again?'

'Maybe.'

'Try to remember as clearly as you can. Did your father shout anything?'

'I was playing football.'

'With him?'

'On my own.'

'Where exactly?'

'There.' I pointed in the direction of the rocks and the beach.

'And then?'

'Nothing.'

'So after you played football you did nothing?'

I shook my head.

'And where was your father at this point?'

'Over by the towels.'

'And then he went for a swim?'

I wanted to say something, but other words kept getting in the way.

'Was anyone else there?'

'Just us.'

'Your neighbour?'

'No.'

He clicked his pen but he still hadn't written anything down. I needed to look at something solid and hold onto it with my eyes. The table. A wall. A block of concrete would be best. 'He was a white shape underwater.'

Johan nodded.

'After a while I couldn't see him anymore.'

'And then he was gone?'

Mum swung the door open.

'Mrs Hammermann, would you please stay in the hall just a moment longer?'

'You know all you need to know.'

'Madam, please!'

'You've already heard all this from me, haven't you?'

They glared at each other.

'Fair enough,' he sighed. 'Let's leave it at that for now.'

He clicked his pen and scribbled the word *Drowning* inside a big box on the form. One word in an expanse of white. 'Your son has been a big help.' He handed Mum his pen. 'Could you sign here, please?'

She left a jagged scribble on the line he'd been pointing at. I noticed he'd spelled my name wrong: *Michael*.

'Are there any other family members?'

'Why?'

'Parents still alive? Brothers or sisters?'

'Only my mother, I think. We're not on speaking terms.'

Johan nodded.

'Circumstances,' said Mum. 'It's personal.'

'Yes, naturally.'

'Why do you ask?'

'A formality. Only asking because we might be able to help track people down, inform them.'

'The only person you need to track down is my husband.'

'If you need any help at all, please contact us.' He shook Mum's hand and then mine. 'All the very best. I, or one of my colleagues, will be in touch if there are any developments.' He put on his cap and left the house without a backward glance. On the quay he said something to one of the other policemen, who was trying to clean the portholes with a dirty rag. Johan stepped over the rail, went into the cabin, and emerged with a new set of papers in his hand. He strode up to Karl's house, knocked on the door, and took a step back.

After waiting a while, he knocked again. The curtains stayed closed. He hunched his shoulders and walked off under the overhanging branches in the front garden. When he reappeared round the other side of the house, he knocked on the door again. Karl didn't open. Johan leaned against the wall with his papers and wrote something on them, then folded them in half and slid them under the door. On his way past Karl's cutter he gave the bow a couple of thumps.

The boy from the police boat had trouble undoing the knots cos I'd done such a good job of fastening them. I hoped Johan would notice and take me with him from now on to tie their ropes.

They sailed slowly out of the bay. I ran upstairs so I could follow them for a while through my binoculars. The sky was as grey as the sea. A container ship crawled across the horizon.

9

Within the hour, Karl was standing in our kitchen. He'd come in without knocking. 'Look what I found.' He held up a plastic bag and let it fall. It thudded onto the table with a sound like overripe fruit. 'Go on, take a look inside.'

Dark-red liquid pooled along the seams. An image of a

shrunken dad flashed into my mind. I bit my tongue so hard I felt dizzy and light-headed. Mum looked away from the bag. Her pale feet stroked the tiled floor.

It was all taking too long for Karl's liking. He thrust his hands into the rustling plastic bag and pulled out a grey, headless fish. 'For you,' he said proudly, only looking at Mum. 'Look.' He showed off the cod from all sides. 'Fattest of the lot.' He grinned and tried to catch her eye. 'Still swimming a few hours ago.'

'Thanks,' I said.

'I've already gutted and scaled it for you.' Karl let the fish slide back into the bag. 'Boys in blue have anything to report? I noticed you had a visitor.'

'He talked to Mum and then to me.'

'Ah.'

'No news,' said Mum.

'One of 'em came knocking on my door but I didn't answer. A pile of forms never found anyone.'

'That's what Mum thought,' I said.

'And right you are,' Karl said to her, but she didn't respond.

'It's what I thought, too,' I said.

'Last thing I need is someone poking their nose in my business. Uniforms telling me what I can and can't catch, how many of this, how many of that. If fish don't want to wind up dead, they should steer clear of my net. The sea's big enough.'

'Now they're looking in the currents,' I said.

'That's all they can do.'

'That's what Johan said, too.'

'Who?'

'The policeman.'

'Aha.'

Mum's jaw clamped tight, as if she was chewing on

something she couldn't bite through.

'Never mind,' said Karl and scratched the corner of his eye. 'I'll be off, then.'

The clock on the cooker said nearly eight o'clock. Time for Dad to listen to the news on the radio. Now that Mum and I were alone, the kitchen seemed smaller, as if there wasn't enough room for both of us to breathe. I retreated into the big armchair with my atlas and ran my finger along the dark-blue arrows in the water.

Twilight shrank the world outside. The evening gave me a kind of hope. If only we could fall asleep, something unexpected might happen. If not while we slept, then tomorrow. Yes, tomorrow! I could feel it tingling in my chest already. 'Tomorrow' sounded like a day that would bring something new. 'Today' didn't, but that was all right, cos today was nearly over.

'Where are you going?'

I had laid the atlas aside and was on my way to the toilet.

'Don't leave,' she said.

'I'm only going for a pee.'

'Stay here. Please.' She sank into a chair and pulled me to her. Her hug squeezed the breath out of me. 'With me,' she whispered. 'Stay here with me.' Her thumb stroked the hollow of my neck till it began to burn.

10

Behind our house was a gently sloping field. To reach it, I had to squeeze through a tangled hedge of brambles.

Thorns pulled loops in my trousers and scratched my hands. The knee-high grass beyond was wet and yellow-ish. It hid moss-covered boulders, speckly like mould.

From the highest point in the field, you could look out over the whole island. Between the trees in front of me was the top of our chimney. Next to it, the quay. Further to the right was the gutter that ran along the roof of Karl's house, and the rusty shed where he kept his catch. The sea was smooth all the way to the horizon.

'Dad!' I shouted. 'DAD!' My voice sounded hoarse.

'DA-AAD!' I looked through my binoculars. 'DAAAAAAAAAAD!'

Our little beach was sheltered by a row of broad-shouldered spruce trees that grew on the spot where a holiday cottage once stood. Now, an overgrown hedge and scorched, mossy foundations were all that was left. It had burned down before Mum and Dad and I came to live here. In among the tall weeds I had once found a rusty metal ashtray and a knife without a handle. I gave the ashtray to Dad. He thought it was funny that the only thing left of a burned-down cottage was an ashtray. I didn't say anything about the knife.

The back of the island started to the right of the burned-down cottage. We called our side the front cos it was where we lived. There were other islands over our horizon, and Dad told me we all belonged together in the same group. Beyond that was the mainland, but the weird thing was that it was an island, too.

If you sailed from the back of the island and kept going long enough, you'd end up at the South Pole. The only building on that side of the island was Miss Augusta's house. We still called it her house, though it wasn't really anybody's anymore.

I walked down the slope and wormed my way backward through the brambles with my hands in my pockets and my hood up. The path I came out on led to Miss Augusta's house. Hardly anyone walked down this way anymore, and the grass had grown over bits of the path. With every step I tried to flatten it down as much as I could.

Gulls were hanging in the air around the house. They screeched to warn one another I was coming. I knew they wouldn't peck me, but I kept my head down anyway. Some of them were lined up along the gutter. One had a mussel in its beak and was trying to crack it open. To be on the safe side, I held my binoculars by the cord so I could swing them like a wrecking ball if any of the gulls ventured too close.

Dad used to call me a cowardy-custard. To him, the gulls were sky sailors. 'Those birds glide for hours on the wind without moving a muscle, and eat what other animals leave lying around. Magnificent, lazy creatures. They live without wasting any energy at all.'

'They're screechy and scary.'

'You'd better check your underpants, Mikael. There might be a brown stripe down the middle.'

'Is not.'

'Just look at that beak. Mouth, hands, and a weapon, all in one.'

All I could see was the nasty hook at the end of it.

'Go on... look.'

I didn't want to get any closer.

'What's the matter?'

'They look so evil.'

'It's people you need to be afraid of, not animals. As long as you can get your hands around their neck, you've nothing to fear.'

'But my hands fit around your neck, don't they?'

'And are you afraid of me?'

I shook my head.

'Well then.'

I still didn't want anything to do with gulls, especially when I was on my own.

I peered at the house through my binoculars. Weeds were sprouting from the gutter. The wooden door was so warped, it refused to close. The handle slammed ominously against the boards that covered the outside wall.

'DAD!'

No answer.

'DAD!' If he'd been hiding in there, he would surely have heard me by now. I picked up a stone and threw it onto the roof. A few gulls took off in fright, others just flapped their wings. 'ARE YOU THERE?'

I stood still. Without Dad, I didn't have the nerve to get any closer, never mind go inside. Slates blown from the roof lay broken in the tall grass. The windows were clouded with sea salt.

Dad had gone over to clean the windows of the empty house once, ladder balanced on his right shoulder and a steaming bucket of soapy water in his other hand. It was one of the chores he used to do for Miss Augusta when she was still alive, and he felt odd about not doing it anymore. 'Soft bugger,' Mum scoffed.

'Just sprucing things up a bit,' said Dad. 'Where's the harm in that?'

I wanted to help, and he let me carry the bucket. By the time we reached her house, half the water had slopped over the rim.

Dad wiped down the windows with the shammy and I sat on a rock and watched him.

Afterward, we walked through the house to make sure everything inside was as it should be. I wasn't allowed to touch anything, but Dad was. Dust had gathered into fluff balls under the chairs and settee, and in the corners of the living room. A gull had found its way inside and couldn't find its way out again. We scared it as much as it scared us.

The longer Miss Augusta was dead, the more empty spaces appeared in her cupboards. When Mum thought Dad had something to make up for, he would go over and look for a present to give her. She'd never say exactly what it was he'd done wrong.

The presents Dad gave Mum had to be selected with great care. It was like looking for medicine without knowing what the illness was. You had to keep trying till you found something that worked. Sometimes it would turn out to be something she could share with us. Other times, it was something to make her look pretty. One of the presents had been a white tablecloth with only one or two burn holes in it. Another time, it was a candleholder with two naked angels standing on one leg and holding a candle each. At times, Dad tried to keep one step ahead of her mood and surprise her with silver earrings, or the like. By now, most of Miss Augusta's jewellery had found its way onto Mum's bedside table. The necklace with the sparkling blue stones was the only real prize left in the deserted house.

On one of our present-hunts, I had taken the blue necklace out of its case and gone downstairs with it. Dad was standing over by the bookcase, running his finger along the spines of the books.

'What about this?'

He turned toward me and smiled when he saw the

necklace. 'I'm saving that one for another time.'

'It's so blue and beautiful.'

'Exactly.'

'Then why not give it to her?'

'It's too beautiful for now. Be a good boy and put it back.'

He pulled open drawers, rummaged around inside, and slid them shut. Pursing his lips, he picked up the framed photograph on the side table and put it down again almost immediately.

I went into the kitchen. The wild flowers in the vase on the table had been dead so long it was impossible to tell what kind of flowers they had once been. They crumbled to the touch. The inside of the vase had turned white, as if someone had drunk buttermilk from it. Karl must have needed a new u-bend, cos it had disappeared from under the sink. The brown gunge at the bottom of the kitchen cupboard had dripped onto the floor.

'And this?'

I held up a bread knife I'd found in a corner cupboard.

'That's a bread knife,' Dad said.

'There's a mixer in here, as well.'

'I can't just give her any old thing, Mikael.'

'But this isn't any old thing, is it?'

'I need to find something else for Mum.'

'Well, what do you need to make up for?'

He raised his eyebrows. 'If only I knew.'

'I like the knife. It's shiny and it's sharp.'

'A bread knife doesn't make a good present.'

'What kind of sorry-present are you looking for?'

'One I can hang on your big red nose, Mikael Hammermann!'

Dad ended up giving her the bread knife after all. He handed it over while I was still hopping around on the doormat, struggling to pull off my boots.

'Aw!' I heard Mum's surprised voice coming from the kitchen. 'For me?'

'For you,' Dad answered.

'That's sweet of you.'

'Bound to come in handy, I reckoned.'

He didn't mention it was me who'd found the present. But when I heard the reassuring sound of their kiss, I didn't mind so much.

It wasn't that I didn't believe Miss Augusta was dead. It was just that, right now, without Dad at my side I couldn't be sure anymore. I was afraid she'd suddenly appear behind me while I was going through her kitchen cupboards or, worse still, when I was on my knees beside her bed trying to poke something out from under the blanket of dust with one of her knitting needles. I pictured two legs silently appearing in the doorway, stockings pulled up tight over a delta of blue veins.

I was even scared to peek in through the windows in case her face suddenly appeared behind the dull pane, with no specs and sunken cheeks. She died without her teeth in. They were still there in a glass on the washbasin, waiting for her.

Dad had found her at the bottom of the stairs. It had been raining for days, and he had gone over with a pot of soup. They didn't tell me what had happened till the next morning. 'Her leg was bent in three places,' Mum said. Dad used a twig to show me what it looked like. 'There's no need for that,' Mum hissed.

While I slept, Karl had taken Miss Augusta across to town in his boat. When he came back that afternoon,

Dad went straight over to see him. He made me stay indoors, so I spied on them from behind the curtain. Karl scratched his head and pointed at his legs. Dad asked him something else. Karl pointed to his boat and flapped his hand about. Dad nodded and patted Karl on the arm.

In the evening, Dad called the hospital on the mainland. Miss Augusta was in their system, but they couldn't tell him much. The next day we were no wiser. Unfortunately, the patient was unable to come to the phone. Three days later it was the same story. They told us not to keep calling, and said they would contact us.

When we hadn't heard anything for ten days, Dad called again. At reception it took them a while to remember who Pernille Augusta was. 'I'll wait,' he told the receptionist.

'They're looking for her file,' he whispered to us with his hand over the mouthpiece.

'Yes, I'm still here... Augusta. That's right.'

Mum leaned against the doorpost and held me close. Dad repeated some of what they said for our benefit. 'About two weeks ago, that's right.'

'A-U-G-U-S-T-A.'

'Yes, we've called before.' Dad pulled a funny face. It made me laugh, but Mum's face didn't so much as twitch.

'They've found her,' he whispered to us.

Silence.

'There's a cross next to her name. Sadly, that means Miss Augusta has passed away.' It was only when he repeated the words to us that he realized what he'd said. 'What did you say?' He sank slowly into his chair as he asked what had happened and why they hadn't informed us, even though they'd promised to. He asked where Miss Augusta was now, and why she'd been buried so quickly, and said no, we weren't family, and yes, he understood that it wasn't her fault, but they might at least have called us. He didn't repeat what the receptionist said.

Once he had hung up, he sat motionless in his chair, staring blankly into space. Mum laid a hand against his neck and sighed.

She gave another sigh, deeper this time, and looked at me. She wanted me to make myself scarce. I pretended to go all the way up to my bedroom in the attic, but instead I sat down at the top of the stairs where I could hear everything. Pernille had been buried the day before at some cemetery or other. Dad had forgotten the name. It began with an S. 'Shu... Sho... Something like that.' The hospital didn't know whether anyone had attended the funeral. 'Seems it's all done by the council, if there's no family or next of kin.'

The hospital had said he could call again to ask for more details of the cemetery. Maybe even speak to a doctor to find out exactly what had happened.

Dad kept going on about the stupid cross next to her name, and that she might have lain there at the bottom of the stairs in the cold for days before he'd found her. He said it was all his fault. Mum said it wasn't, but Dad said yes it was, cos that was how he felt about it.

'They asked if we knew of any relatives.'

'Goodness, no.'

'Me neither.'

'No one.'

'Karl!' Mum blurted out.

'My God... yes.'

'He won't have heard yet, either.'

After hanging around for a while, Dad went over to see him. I sneaked out through the back door and hid among the bushes by the quay.

Karl already knew. The hospital had called him.

'What?'

'Last week.'

'Why didn't you say anything?'

'I thought you would've heard, too.'

'You might at least have come over...'

'Well,' said Karl. 'Can't change that now.' He bent down, turned on his outside tap, rinsed his dirty hands, and then wiped them off on his trousers, which only made them dirty again. 'She was a fine woman,' he said. 'At first they thought I was family.'

'And?'

'I said no, and sharpish like. No way I was going to foot the bill. D'you know what a funeral costs these days?'

'You might at least have told us. We live on the same island!'

'And... are you family? Were you ready to get yer wallet out?'

'No, but we were neighbours. I was fond of her. How much trouble would it have been for you to come and see us?'

'Well, now you know.'

'I mean, wasn't she your...'

'My what?'

'You know... didn't you two... for a while?'

'Listen, Hammermann. I'm not coughing up good money for a corpse, don't care whose it is. No one's laying this at my door. She's lying in a council grave somewhere. One grave's as cold as the next. She'd be no better off elsewhere. And if you're so keen to part with yer money, give them a call and tell them where to send the bill. Leave me out of it. I've got enough on my plate.'

'Take it easy. I only thought because you two once...'

'That's no business of yours, Hammermann.'

'But you were together, weren't you?'

'For a while.'

'So it's not like you were strangers...'

'Who are you to tell me what to feel?'

'That's not what I'm saying.'

'Well, shut up about it then.'

Dad held up his hands as if Karl had pointed a gun at him.

Karl marched down to his cutter. 'I've got things to do.'

That evening, Dad got the torch out and went over to Miss Augusta's to close the windows, turn off the power and the water mains, and to wedge the crooked front door shut.

He came back with a houseplant under each arm, and banged the front door with his elbow so I would open it for him. He put the plant pots down on the table. Grains of soil fell out, dry as mince that's been stirred round the pan for too long. Mum swept them into her hand and told me to fetch two old plates from the cupboard to put under the pots. Dad produced a shiny hairpin from his trouser pocket.

'For you,' he said to Mum.

'What do you mean?'

'From the lost and found. Now it's yours.'

'Mine?' A pink shell was stuck to the head of the pin. 'That belongs to Pernille,' Mum said indignantly.

'And now it belongs to you.'

'You had no right to touch it.'

'It's no one's, not anymore.'

She went to give him back the hairpin, but Dad turned to put our new plants on the windowsill and started plucking out the yellow leaves. They curled and caught fire as he threw them on the burning wood in the fire-place.

'I really don't want it.'

Dad hid his hands behind his back when she tried to give him her present a second time.

Next morning she wore her hair up, held in place by a shiny hairpin with a pink shell.

11

I tore the middle pages out of my notebook, the one with the lined paper, sat down at my desk, and started to write a letter. *Where are you? Where are you? Where are you?* I wrote in one long wavy line at the top of the page. *Dad, Dad, Dad. When are you coming back? I've looked for you everywhere. Mum too. The police came and Karl's been out looking too. DadDadDadDad.* I wrote and wrote till the whole page was full. In the very bottom corner there was just enough room to write *Sorry.* As soon as I'd written it, I crossed it out again. Stupid word. That's what you say when you want to get away with something. I kept the start of *Sorry* and turned it into *Sorrow,* but that wasn't right, either. I scribbled *My fault* over the top. You could hardly read it, but it was still there. I was to blame.

I rolled up the letter till it was thin enough to slide into the bottle. I plugged it with a cork, picked up one of the stones from my collection on the windowsill, and tapped the cork till it was snug inside the neck.

The letter was rolled up with the writing on the outside. A stranger might have trouble reading it through the uneven surface of the glass, but Dad knew my handwriting. He'd taught it to me himself.

I climbed over the barnacle-pocked boulders to a pointed rock that jutted six or seven feet out into the sea. It was the rock I must 'never-never-never—look at me when I'm talking to you—never ever jump off.' Cross my heart and hope to die.

I kept as far from the water as I could so the waves couldn't snatch at my feet. Even at the spot where the sea was calmer, I was too scared to go right to the edge. Gaping monster jaws lay waiting in the deep.

As far out as I dared, I took the bottle from my coat pocket, pressed a kiss to the green glass, and hurled it with all my might. It disappeared with a splash, but luckily it resurfaced and started bobbing lopsidedly along. Now it was up to the sea to pass my letter from wave to wave till it reached Dad. For a moment I was afraid it might smash to pieces against the rocks, but it didn't, and it began to drift steadily away. I tried to keep track, to see where the waves were taking it, but I lost sight of it amid floating clumps of seaweed that were almost the same shade of green.

Then the waiting began.

12

'Time for your bath!' Mum shouted up to me.

'In a minute!' I shouted back.

'Now,' she answered.

'I want to keep looking a bit longer.'

'No.'

Through my binoculars, I was expecting to catch sight of Dad sitting with his back to me, arms around his knees. On a rock or at the place on the beach where he'd left his towel. I even scanned the gulls circling in the air.

'Just another minute? Please?'

'Now means now.' Her words were jagged round the edges.

I sat my backside down on the cold metal of the empty bath and turned the tap on as far as it would go. The water thundered. It made my willy float like a buoy as it crept up to my belly button and my knees.

Suddenly the stream of water stopped. Something was stuck in the tap. Before I could stick my finger in to feel what it was, a tiny figure tumbled out. He was still wearing his swimming trunks.

'Dad!'

He dived deep into the bathwater and surfaced next to the island my tummy made. I helped him up with my finger and kept the island as still as I could. He lay stretched out, panting. He could fit both feet inside my belly button.

'You've gone all little,' I said, once he had caught his breath. We laughed, and the shaking of my tummy almost sent him skidding back into the water.

'Where have you been?'

He shrugged.

'Did you get my letter?'

Pressing thumb and forefinger together, he pulled an invisible zip across his lips.

'Can't you talk anymore?'

He shook his head.

'But you got my letter?'

He nodded.

'Are you angry?'

He shook his head again.

'Mum's been looking for you. Me too. And the police, and Karl.'

He splashed water at me. It went in my eyes, but right now I didn't mind. I wanted to call Mum, but then I decided he had to put on his good clothes first and have a shave. He wouldn't be allowed to kiss her with cactus cheeks. As if he could read my thoughts, he said, 'Don't say anything just yet.'

'So you *can* talk!'

He clamped a startled hand over his mouth. 'No,' he whispered so quietly I could barely hear, and shook his head. Then he zipped his lips again and pointed at me.

'Am I not allowed to say anything?'

He gave me a stern look from beneath his dark eyebrows.

'Not to Mum?'

He gave a curt nod.

'I won't say a thing. Least of all to Mum.' I spat in the bathwater to seal the pledge. 'I swear.'

Dad smiled. He stood up and took a stroll across my tummy. His feet tickled. When he flicked water at me again, I flicked him back. We slapped the water and I made waves with my hands and kicked my feet. It sloshed over the rim of the bath but that didn't stop us.

Suddenly Mum opened the door. 'What's all this?'

Dad vanished instantly.

'Look! The floor is soaking wet.' She felt the bathwater. 'You've been in here much too long.'

As inconspicuously as possible, I groped around behind my back to see if Dad might be hiding there. I couldn't find him.

In a single motion, Mum reached in and pulled the plug.

'Don't!' I pushed her away and accidentally hit her in the stomach.

'What the hell do you think you're doing?' she gasped.

The bathwater was clear and empty. Maybe he had slipped straight through the shiny plughole and had managed to wedge himself tight in the pipe. My little fingers could just fit into the little holes.

'Behave yourself.'

'Wait!' I cried.

'Don't act the goat with me.' She grabbed me roughly by the arm and yanked me to my feet. The plughole slurped and gurgled. Mum began to dry me off, even though I'd been drying myself off for ages now. The rough towel scoured my cheeks and folded my ears this way and that. The red bath mat beneath my feet was dark and cold from the water.

'Look at the mess you've made.'

'Dad started it.'

'What did you say?'

I counted the black tiles on the floor so I wouldn't have to look at her. When I was dry, she handed me the towel. 'Use this to clean up.' She'd forgotten to dry between my toes, so I did that myself.

When I heard her go downstairs, I turned on the tap again very carefully, just far enough for a steady trickle. I put the plug back in so the water would break Dad's fall and stop him landing smack on the hard metal. Nothing except water came from the tap, but I kept watching. It dawned on me that it would take him a while to find his way back into the tap. As long as I was patient, he'd appear all by himself. I stared and stared at the running water.

'What did I just tell you?' Mum had come back upstairs without me noticing.

'To clean up. I'm supposed to clean up.'

'Turn that tap off. Now.'

13

A few days later I put another letter in a bottle and threw it into the sea. Karl was standing on the quay near his house, a mound of fish spread out in front of him. Little fish jumped into the air one after the other, like they'd been jolted by electric shocks.

'Mikael!'

I pretended not to hear him.

'Mi-ka-el!' I peered out from under my hood, and he beckoned me over. I was afraid he'd seen me out on the dangerous rock with my bottle and was going to tell me off, but instead he asked me to help him sort the fish.

'Now?'

'If you like.'

'Okay.'

'You know where they go, right?' Karl pointed to the beaten-up containers all around us. 'Like with like.'

'Yup.'

'If you don't know where a fish belongs, you ask me.' Over and over, he grabbed two or three fish of the same kind by the tail and whacked them into one of the containers. 'Seen that?' Karl nodded toward the faded nets hanging out to dry on the deck of his cutter. 'They're in a bad way.'

'What happened?'

'Dragged 'em way too close to the seabed, searching for your dad.'

'Oh.'

'Should be able to fix most of 'em up.'

I didn't know what to say, so I stared at the ground. There were flounders, whiting, and even a cod. There was another fish, too, one I didn't recognize. It had silver scales that gave off a kind of rainbow sheen and its tailfin was rounded, not pointed. I picked it up and took a good look, then let it fall again cos I didn't want to ask Karl what container to put it in.

'What does she do all day?'

'Who?'

'Your mother.'

'All kinds of things.'

'Does she ever leave the house?'

'Sometimes she goes out searching. She doesn't phone as much anymore.'

'You two surviving over there?'

It felt strange to hear him say 'surviving.'

'Must be tough on you, too.'

'Dunno.'

'The sea's a treacherous bastard. Hard to believe. One minute he's walking around, next minute he's gone.' He shook his head.

A crab scuttled out from beneath the fish, claws raised, dragging a string of seaweed behind it. There was a starfish, too, legs curled up like caterpillars. They hold onto the rocks so tight, you have to peel them off like a plaster.

'D'you fancy goin' out on the cutter with me sometime?'

'How d'you mean?'

'Just a day out on the water. You can give me a hand. Beats sitting around over there all day with yer Mum.'

'Maybe.'

'Up to you.'

Karl fell silent and bent over his catch again. Most of the fish had eyes that were dull and dead. Eyes that could look through salty water without it stinging. Eyes that might have seen my dad. I concentrated on picking out the little fish, and nabbed the crab cos I was allowed to fling it back into the sea. I also found a yellow plastic bottle that must have contained some kind of cleaner. The label had been soaked off.

'You find the strangest things drifting out at sea,' said Karl.

'Ever found a football?'

'A football?'

'A red one made of patches all sewn together.'

'Not that I can remember.'

'It was red.'

'Easy to spot.'

I nodded toward the cove. 'Over that way.'

'No, not that I remember.'

It was a good sign, it seemed to me. If Karl had found the ball without Dad hanging onto it, that would be terrible. This way, Dad and the ball might still be together, and it could help Dad stay afloat.

'Did you lose it a while back?'

'Uh-huh.'

'D'you want a new one?'

'Nope.'

'I could look out for one when I'm in town.'

'No need.'

Karl dug his knuckles into his lower back and stretched.

'My hair's getting long, don't you reckon?'

I shrugged. 'Looks okay to me.'

'I can always tell when it's too long. I get this itch.'

The fish with the rounded tailfin and the rainbow sheen lay between us in a puddle of brownish water. As soon as I picked it up, its gills flapped open and it began to gulp. Its eyes were a deep, staring black. It tensed like a calf muscle, and the spasms almost sent it sliding from my grasp.

The gulping slowed. It looked like it wanted to say something but didn't have enough life left, to repeat something Dad had whispered to its cold and fishy heart, something it was supposed to tell me when it met me. I pressed the smooth scales to my ear, and a shiver burrowed its way from my neck deep inside my body. I heard its mouth open and close, and pressed it closer.

Gills flapping.

Another spasm.

It was trying to tell me! I tightened my grip to stop it slipping out of my hands. Now the words would come.

Now!

The fish fell slack and heavy as an arm that's gone to sleep. Its mouth hung open. I wanted to blow breath into it, to force a heartbeat into its chest with my thumbs, but I was too late.

Stupid fucking fish.

It almost slipped out of my hands. Stupid, shitty, dead fucking fish. I took hold of its tail and flung it back into the sea. It flew through the air in a high arc. The gulls around us on the rocks and the quay flapped open their wings and dived after it, screeching. Watching it disappear, I felt relieved and sad at the same time.

'What did you do that for?'

I turned away so Karl couldn't see me cry.

'Perfectly good fish that was.'

Snot ran down over my top lip.

'It was a stupid fucking dead fish.'

'No need to cry about it.' He placed an uneasy hand on my shoulder. 'It's not that big a deal. You've been a good help.'

I sniffed hard and wiped the snot on my sleeve. 'Didn't say anything.'

'Who didn't?'

'That fish.'

'The fish?' Karl raised his eyebrows. 'The fish didn't say anything. Can't argue with you there.'

Without another word, I ran off.

14

In the dim light of early morning I came down from my attic room to go to the toilet. Secretly, I hoped the noise would wake Mum, and that she'd call to me sleepily, lifting up the covers so I could climb in and curl up beside her with the warmth of her breasts against my back and her arm wrapped tight around me.

As quietly as I could, I eased Mum and Dad's bedroom door open. The lamp on Mum's side of the bed was still on. Her jaw was slack and she sighed as she slept, as if every breath was an effort. I was just about to slink back up to bed when I saw something move under the covers, not much bigger than a mouse. It crawled over Mum's shoulder and came out from under the blanket by her neck.

'Dad!' I said softly. 'You're back.'

He quickly put a finger to his lips and leaned as far forward as he could to see if Mum was still asleep. He had to hang on to her earlobe to stop himself from falling.

'I'll be quiet,' I whispered. 'Are you not talking again?'

He shook his head and hauled away a few strands of hair that had fallen in front of Mum's face. He had to walk across her cheek to do it, but his footsteps didn't wake her.

'Sorry about the bath,' I whispered. 'Mum pulled the plug.'

He didn't seem to hear me.

'I didn't say anything to her.'

Dad looped the strands of hair behind her ear.

'Do you want me to help you?'

Mum smacked her lips and rolled onto her back. Her pillow moved and Dad fell over backward, disappearing among the bedclothes. I wanted to dive over and help him, but I didn't dare get any closer to Mum. I held my breath and stared at the blanket.

Something moved.

Thank goodness. There was Dad climbing along the ridge of her neck. 'Are you going to stay with us forever?' I asked in a whisper.

He stretched and yawned. That made me yawn, and I started him off again.

'I didn't say anything to Mum,' I said again. 'That's what you wanted, wasn't it?'

Struggling to keep his balance, he made his way across Mum's neck and up toward her face. He knelt by the hollow at the base of Mum's throat and curled up inside it, knees tucked against his chest.

'Will you come downstairs together in a while?'

He waved me away with his hand.

'Sleep tight.'

His eyes were already closed.

The catch on the bedroom door clicked as I pulled it shut. Downstairs on the settee, I gathered all the cushions I could find and buried myself under them. This was the best bed ever. Mum always tucked me in like this when I had the flu or if I conked out a few hours before midnight on New Year's Eve.

The hiss and splutter of the coffee machine woke me up. It was already light, and most of the cushions had fallen onto the floor next to the settee. Mum was pacing from one room to another, wearing Dad's raincoat. She coughed as she lit up a cigarette, the last one in the pack. She was trying to get the morning off to a good start, as if the day was a chore she could tackle at a brisk pace, armed with a pail of soapy water. The hollow at the base of her throat was empty. 'Dad came back again last night,' I said, so softly only I could hear.

15

'Perhaps we should get on with this.'

Without asking, Mum had taken my arithmetic book from the cupboard in my bedroom, and now it lay open on the table in front of her.

'Come and sit over here,' she said, scraping back the chair next to her. 'I can try and help you with it for now.'

'No need.' Phlegm caught in my throat, and my voice sounded weird.

'Where did you and Dad leave off?'

I had to swallow a few times. 'In the middle somewhere.'

She opened the book at any old page.

'Here?'

'Too far on.'

She flicked back a bit. 'What about here?'

'Can't remember.' I looked out the window.

'See if you can find it.' She slid the book toward me.

There was a drawing of a smiling dog and a little girl cutting up a birthday cake with the kind of saw you cut down trees with. Dad always let me skip percentages— them, and the chapters about money and interest. The corners of the pages whirred under my thumb as I skimmed back through the book. It was a nice sound, so I did it a few times over.

It felt wrong, Mum and me sitting here with this book.

'I don't know anymore,' I said, snapping the book shut.

'Well then, we'll just pick a place and start there.'

She picked chapter eleven.

'There's no need, honest,' I said. 'I'd rather wait for Dad.'

Half to herself and half out loud, she began to read. 'Chapter eleven, fractions. There's a numerator and a de- nominator and a fraction bar... You can also write the numbers after the decimal point as... Reducing a frac- tion...'

When we hit a sum, she mumbled, 'Let's read every- thing first.' As she got to the end of the page, I turned it over so she could keep on reading. 'Natural numbers are numbers that you know from... Pie charts... made up of various sections that come together...' She came to a sudden halt, as if she'd got stuck in the white space be- tween two words.

'That's where you've got up to,' I pointed. She sniffed but didn't cry. I looked at her sideways.

'Should we stop now?'

She shook her head. 'You read on.'

I did as she said. When we came to the first exercise, I guessed an answer. 'About three and a half.'

She wiped her nose on her jumper, leaving a shiny trail on the sleeve. 'That's right, I think.'

I gave answers for all the sums that came next. Some- times I got them wrong on purpose so she would have something to say, but she didn't correct me once. Her face had melted like a candle.

'Shall I finish it off in my room?'
I shuffled up the stairs.

There was a haze in the air, as if a wire screen had been stretched across my window. The words in the book began to blur cos I'd been staring at them too long. I shaded in a couple of triangles with my pencil and wrote down the answers to a few of the easiest sums.

Four times a year I was sent a pile of tests to check my progress, and at the end of the summer my new textbooks arrived. It was the only post ever addressed to me. They also sent Dad a thin book of 'didactic tips', which he always let me use to light the fire. Dad let me fill in the tests in pencil and allowed me to use my books. 'Knowledge means knowing exactly where to look things up,' he said. Then he'd pick up the rubber and erase all my wrong answers. 'You need to get better at looking stuff up, Mikael.'

Back at my desk I'd fill in the empty boxes with different answers, and he'd go through them again with his rubber. We'd keep on doing it till I had almost everything right. Then he let me put the finished test sheets in the Education Department envelope, and they'd be sent off next time the boat came to bring us our groceries and our post.

A month or so later, word would come back that I had done extremely well on the tests and that I was ahead of most other children my age. The same envelope contained a new batch of tests.

16

Something glinted up at me from between two floor-boards on the landing. I ran upstairs to my room to get my Swiss Army knife. Back on the landing, I pulled out the smallest blade and winkled the shiny object out of the crack: a tiny nugget of gold. It took me a while to recognize it as part of Dad's watch.

'I've found that little thingamajig from your watch.' It was only when I'd shouted it a second time that I froze. 'What is it?' Mum shouted from the kitchen.

'Nothing.'

'Then what were you shouting about?'

'Sorry.'

'Come down here and talk to me if you want to ask me something.'

'I don't want anything.'

It was the little winder from the side of his watch. We'd searched the whole house for it. 'Damn-damn-damn it,' Dad had growled as he crawled across the living room, peering into the cracks under the skirting boards and running his hands along the sides of the settee. He even snipped open the Hoover bag, dissecting its contents like a giant furball.

'Were you fiddling with it?' Mum asked me. 'Is that why it's missing?' I'd done no such thing, but my face turned red anyway. Dad told her she couldn't blame me without good reason, and besides, he reckoned it must have fallen off the watch while he was wearing it. It wasn't long before the hands came to a standstill, and he put it in the drawer of his bedside table, where it had lain ever since.

I crept into their room. The watch was right where Dad had left it. It shone up at me, its hands pointing to a few minutes past four. As soon as I picked it up, the second hand began to tick all by itself. Holding it to my ear, I could hear the clockwork shifting and shuffling. Not even half a minute later, it fell still again. I fitted the gold nugget back onto the side and started winding. I'd never even seen a photo of my grandad, but I knew he'd won this watch playing cards in a pub. When he died it was passed on to Dad, and when Dad died it would belong to me. Dad told me all this when I was sitting on his lap one day and he let me take the watch off his wrist.

I turned the winder till it wouldn't go any further. Grey dirt lined the metal ridges. I tried to put the watch on, but my wrist was too skinny even for the last hole in the strap. The shiny back of its face felt cold against my skin. I slipped it back into Dad's bedside table.

17

'He's here to see you.'

'To see me?' I couldn't help but smile. Usually Karl only came over to see Dad or to have his hair cut.

I went to the front door. Mum shuffled along behind me, but hung back in the shadow of the hallway.

'Hey, Karl.'

'Hey, young fella.'

'Bagged yourself another whale?' It was what Dad always said to him, so I thought I'd say it, too.

'Nope, no whales this time, sad to say.'

'If you net yourself a treasure chest, you'll give your neighbour a cut, won't you?'

'Uh... I s'pose.'

'That's a deal, then.' Dad always whacked him on the shoulder at this point, but I reckoned that would just be weird, coming from me.

'I've got something for you,' Karl continued.

'For me?'

It was only now I noticed he was holding something behind his back.

'I was in town the other day.'

'So, what is it?'

He held out his present. I jumped.

'My ball?'

Karl gave a satisfied nod.

This football was red, too, but the hexagonal patches were fake, printed on.

'That's not mine.'

'They had all sorts.' Karl bounced the ball on the floor a few times. 'I've already pumped it up for you.'

'I don't want this one.'

'You don't want it?'

'No.'

'But you lost your old one, didn't you?'

Mum came and stood next to me. 'You lost your ball? The one you got for your birthday?'

'Did not,' I said fiercely, but my voice sounded squeakier than I wanted it to. 'It's upstairs under my bed.'

Karl pointed over his shoulder to the quay. 'The other day on that very spot you told me you'd lost your ball.'

'Did not,' I huffed.

'All right, whatever you say. Anyway, I bought this ball and it's for you.' He pressed it into my hands. 'Here you are.'

The thing smelled of new raincoats. 'I don't want it, honest.'

'Remind me to buy you a present again sometime.'

'Here.' I tried to give him the ball back, but he raised his hands in refusal.

'If you don't like it, you can always kick it into the sea.' Karl tried to catch Mum's eye. 'I thought I'd bring back something nice for the boy, and this is the thanks I get.'

She turned and walked upstairs.

'I didn't lose my ball,' I said, loud enough so she could still hear me.

'Cheers, then.' Karl tapped two fingers against the side of his head. 'I'll leave you both to it.'

I closed the front door and shot after Mum, afraid she'd go looking for the ball under my bed. 'I think it must be in the shed,' I said as breezily as I could.

'Have you lost it?'

'No, I'll go and get it in a bit.'

'You do that. I'm going for a pee.'

The latch on the bathroom door squeaked when she turned it. Seconds later I heard hissing and splashing in the toilet bowl.

Up in my room, I rolled the new ball into a dark corner under my bed, so if Mum came looking she might mistake it for my old one.

'You're going to have a baby brother,' Dad had said, stroking his big round belly. 'Your Dad's expecting.'

I pounded the bump a couple of times with my fists. 'Steady on,' he said, holding up his hands to protect it. 'Mum didn't want to have another baby, so I'm doing the honours. You're going to have a little brother.'

'Or a little sister?'

'Would you rather have a sister?'

'One of each would be nice.'

'Now you're asking too much.'

'All right then, a little brother.'

Dad pretended to have a terrible stomach ache. 'Baby's on its way. Take my hand and hold on tight, Mikael.' It was the quickest delivery ever. Within seconds he'd given birth to a bright red football that bounced across the carpet.

'There you go,' he gasped, exhausted. 'What do you want to call him?'

'My ball?'

'Not much of a name, is it?'

'I didn't mean that.'

'What then?'

'Uuh... just "Ball", I think.'

'Up to you,' said Dad. 'Right now, it's time for a smoke. Well deserved after all that hard labour.'

I didn't let on that I'd already spotted the ball when it arrived in our grocery crates. Nor did I tell him I knew I'd soon be getting a remote-controlled boat, cos I'd found it on top of the cupboard behind the row of encyclopaedias, and that it ran on those pricey square batteries we didn't have, and that it wasn't really the boat I'd been hoping for anyway. That was okay, though, cos I'd had lots of time to practise being over the moon with it, so I already knew what to say to make them think they'd bought exactly the right one.

18

On my own I managed to eat okay, but with Mum sitting across from me I couldn't, even if my stomach was as empty as a deserted fox den. Every mouthful caught in my throat like a pile of dead twigs.

After supper, Mum took my plate. 'Are you finished, too?'

'Yes.'

She tipped her plate and scraped her macaroni on top of mine with her fork. 'Toss this up on top of the shed.'

'Are you sure?' She usually turned up her nose if Dad chucked leftovers from supper or stale bits of bread up there.

'Bring back some briquettes, will you?'

The wind was rustling among the trees. I stood on the garden bench so I could see over the edge, and dumped the macaroni on the corrugated iron roof. Dad always said he'd rather feed the gulls than the rats that foraged in the dustbin.

Silhouettes came swooping in from all sides, screeching, flapping, and crowding one another out. Within seconds the first gulls had snatched away the biggest chunks and flown up to the ridge of our roof to gobble them down undisturbed.

Flying shitbags, I thought as I looked up at them from a safe distance, but without Dad around I felt like I was being nasty. Sky sailors, I told myself, they're sky sailors. I inched open the shed door and inhaled the familiar smell of petrol. When Dad used his chainsaw, that smell hung around his jumper for days. It took a while for my eyes to get used to the shed's dark insides. A mouse darted away along the edge of a cupboard. Ropes hung from the walls, along with the sun lounger, Dad's axe, and coils of garden hose. A mist of cobwebs floated between them. The chair Dad always insisted he was going to repair soon was standing where it had stood for years, surrounded by rakes, plastic watering cans, and a tower of brown flower pots.

Above me I could hear the ticking of the gulls walking to and fro on the metal roof and pecking at the leftover macaroni. A half-finished birdhouse was clamped in the vice on Dad's cluttered workbench. I found the paper sack with the briquettes on the floor beside the bench. Creepy-crawlies wriggled away in all directions when I lifted it up. There were three whole briquettes left inside, along with a few loose bits and pieces.

I was just about to leave when I caught sight of him, staring up at me from under the workbench. I gave a start and the sack fell out of my hands. 'Dad?' His wet hair was plastered against his scalp, sticking up here and there. He was shivering, still wearing only his swimming trunks. 'How long have you been sitting here?' I swallowed once or twice. 'Why do you keep disappearing?'

He looked smaller than when I'd seen him on Mum's bed. 'Mum misses you. So do I. You have to stay, you really do. You have to stay with us now.'

He raised his arm slowly and stabbed a finger in my direction.

'What is it?' I shook my head. 'What do you mean?'

He kept on pointing.

'Don't do that.' I went down on my knees and crawled under the workbench. 'Come on. I'll help you.' The closer I came, the smaller he got. 'Come here.' I tried to grab him but he crawled away and hid behind the cupboard. I began to pull at it with all my strength, and a gap appeared between the cupboard and the wall. 'Don't be afraid,' I whispered reassuringly. 'You have to stay. I'll help you.'

My hand could just about fit into the gap, but my arm couldn't. I hung from the cupboard with my full weight, and it began to tilt forward. Planks creaked and it hit the ground with a bang. Like a rat driven from its hiding place, Dad shot back behind the drawers of his work-bench. I dived toward him and felt his feet brush softly against my fingers, but he slipped away. 'Please Dad, don't be scared. You need to put on a jumper and sit by the fire. Come on. It's time I gave you to Mum.'

I wanted to crawl onto his lap and bury my face in the warmth of his armpit. I'd let him tickle me till I choked. I wanted to stick my head up his jumper and lose myself under there and feel the hair on his belly brush my cheek.

I felt tears welling up. I pulled at the leg of the work-bench, but it wouldn't give an inch. 'Dad, come on. Please.' Leaning over the worktop, I could just see down behind it. I saw a pale shape, the glimmer of two tiny eyes. 'I have to give you back to Mum,' I whispered. The pale shape grew vaguer, till only two gleaming dots re-mained.

Then they disappeared, too.

The darkness grew dizzyingly deep.

19

That night I saw every hour pass. Still, I must have fallen asleep, cos suddenly it was morning. I blinked at my alarm clock. Eight o'clock precisely. An hour and a half of empty dreams at most, cos I'd seen six-thirty come and go. My knees wobbled when I got up. My heart was pounding in my ears, so loud Mum would be sure to hear it if I got too close to her. I steered clear.

The radio in the kitchen said it was Thursday, the day Brigitta brings our groceries. We didn't know what Brig-itta was really called. That was the name welded in rusted letters to the bow of his boat. Mostly we called him 'the grocery man.'

I already had my raincoat on as I peered through the window. He was later than usual. Then his horn sounded, three short blasts in a row, and his boat turned into the bay. I went outside with our empty grocery crates.

'Wait!' Mum shouted.

'He's here!' I called back.

'Come back for a sec.'

In the kitchen, all the cupboard doors were open. Mum pressed a piece of paper to the wall and scribbled on it.

'You'd better be quick,' I said, tapping my shoe against the table leg.

'Stop that. Brigitta's only just got here.' She shot a glance at the towers of tinned food and packets of macaroni and scrawled something else on the paper before folding it in half. 'Here, run.'

Brigitta was already standing with one foot on the quay and the other on the deck of his boat. 'Hiya!' I shouted above the din of the engine. He nodded. His head seemed to be moulded from the same clay as Karl's, but his face was pitted so badly it looked like someone had started chewing on it but had given up cos it was too tough. His hand went up to the corner of his mouth, took a stub of cigarette between two fingers, and fired it into the water. I handed him our crates. Brigitta took them, shuffled over to the open hatch on the deck, and clattered them down inside. He disappeared down the ladder after them and lifted three full crates up onto the deck.

Every second week he brought our order. Much of it was the same: tomato sauce, tins of yellowish mushrooms and peas mixed with carrots, a pack of sanitary towels, sweets like lumps of coloured glue, flour, rice, a carton of cigarettes, coffee, two boxes of cereal, briquettes, and a few toilet rolls. Once in a while there were razor blades for Dad, matches, socks, or chocolate that had already turned whitish. The socks were always way too big so they were sure to fit us.

With his foot, Brigitta nudged the crates ahead of him toward the rail. 'Thur y'ago.' He wore gloves with the fingertips snipped off. He handed me the leather pouch that contained our post, along with a couple of newspapers for Dad.

'I'm sorry 'bout yer father,' he said suddenly. 'Tough on yer mother, too.'

I didn't know what to say. He got a mumbled thanks.

From the breast pocket of his dirty apron he took a pouch of tobacco and began to roll a cigarette. I held out our shopping list. 'From my mother.'

'Wait a sec.' He rolled the filled paper between his fingers, licked the edge, and clamped the unlit cigarette between his lips.

'Give it here.' He took the note from my hand. 'As long as thur's no funny fruit on it.' He always said that when Dad handed him our shopping list. As he went through our order, his mouth read along soundlessly. He took a quick look at the back, too. Blank. 'That's not much,' he sighed. 'Where's yer mother?'

'My mother?'

'Mmmm.'

'Indoors.'

His chin jutted in the direction of our house.

'D'you want me to fetch her?'

'You do that.'

Mum was still sitting there in her dressing gown. She jumped when I knocked on the window and signalled for her to come.

'Why?'

'The grocery man wants you for something.'

'What?'

I shrugged and went back to Brigitta. They hadn't met all that often. Dad always had the empty grocery crates ready and waiting, and I usually helped him. Mum was in charge of the lists.

Dressing gown flapping, Mum followed me down, her bare feet midway between a walk and a run. 'Have you heard something?' she shouted, halfway along the quay. Brigitta's gaze avoided her bare legs. Just as well she had knickers on. 'You wanted to see me?'

'Terrible news 'bout yer husband.' He reached out his hand. She shook it briefly.

'Have you seen something?'

'Sorry.'

'Pardon?'

'Sorry for yer loss.'

'We still don't know anything,' she said, her voice shrill.

Brigitta breathed in as he said 'Naw.' He fished a lighter from his breast pocket. Dad's cigarettes smelled different, but this smell was nice, too.

'It wuz on the radio.'

'What?'

''Bout yer husband.'

'When?'

'When it happened.'

'What did they say?'

'The usual. Standard report.'

'Did they mention a name?'

'Call 'im b' name? Naw.'

'Colin Ba-what?'

'He means they didn't mention it,' I said.

'Well?'

'Missing person, that's all.'

'That's all?'

'Said thur wuz a drownin' in these parts.'

'Drowning?' Mum's voice cracked.

'Nuthin' anyone can do.'

'They all say they've done everything they can.'

'That's what they always say.'

'Meantime, we still don't know where he is.'

'The sea's a big place.'

I wanted him to say something else. That sometimes people are found weeks later, tired and hungry but alive out in the middle of the ocean. That they're only lost for a while.

Mum pointed toward the cove. 'That's where he went in.' Brigitta nodded and looked at the spot.

'We've looked all over. The police were here. Nothing. Coastguard. No one, nothing. My husband might never come back.'

A thud echoed in my chest. 'You're not allowed to say that,' I said.

'Please can you keep an eye out for him? Please.'

She took Brigitta's hand.

'Can do.'

'It's our only hope.'

''Course I can,' sighed Brigitta. 'But... you know...'

'But what?'

Brigitta shrugged his shoulders. 'It's already been more than a week.'

'Ten days,' I said, before Mum could.

'Eleven,' Mum corrected. 'Today makes eleven.'

'Eleven days?' Brigitta raised his eyebrows and began to nod. It was the nodding people do when something is clear, clear as can be.

'That's all you need to know.'

'What is?' Mum and I said in unison.

'That he's down wi' the eels.' In a flash, Mum's hand struck his face. For an instant there was silence. Even the boat's engine seemed to stutter. Brigitta eyed her with all the emotion of a goat.

'You can shut your ugly face,' she barked.

'After eleven days, it's no use.'

She hit him again. This time he swayed back and she mainly caught his nose. 'Are you deaf?'

Brigitta felt at his nose.

'I said keep that stinking gob of yours shut.'

He took the cigarette between his fingers, licked a thread of tobacco from his lip, and swallowed it. 'I'm tellin' you how it is.'

Mum was ready to lash out again, but he'd already taken a step back.

'Get out of here,' Mum screamed. 'Go!'

Brigitta didn't quite know what to do, but when Mum grabbed stones from the ground and began to hurl them at him, he bolted for his cabin. One of the stones cracked a porthole.

'Piss off!' she shrieked.

The engine made the boat tremble. The small funnel huffed dark clouds of diesel smoke.

'I never want to see you here again.' Mum stamped and spat, her eyes red-rimmed. 'You're to blame!' she screamed at Brigitta. The drone of the engine was so loud, there was no way he could hear her.

'Mum-mum-mum-mum, please.' I wrapped my hand around hers and tried to smooth her crooked fingers. She shook her hand fiercely till I let go. Her wild movements loosened the cord of her dressing gown. Goose pimples dotted her pale skin and her breasts swung with every word she screamed.

The boat had turned and was already a few yards offshore.

'Mum!' I begged. 'Stop, stop, stop.' Her arms flailed in empty space. Her fingers clawed the air. Then she spun round and stormed toward the house.

Inside, she flung the drying rack aside. The standard lamp slammed to the floor, its shade snapped off, and the exposed bulb burned like a glowing kernel. In one sweep, she sent our plates and the half-full teapot crashing from the draining board.

'Don't Mum. Don't do that,' I begged her. 'Dad will come back again.'

She charged toward me, her eyes full of tears. 'Then tell me when, Mikael. Where? It's not true.'

'But I saw him in the bath, and in your bed, and in the shed.'

'You're lying!'

'I'm not, I'm not.'

'You have to give me something to hope for, Mikael!' she yelled. 'Please. Say something, anything, to give me hope.'

She grabbed at her hair hysterically, tearing out whole tufts and holding them in front of her as if they were meant for me. 'Dad's dead!' she howled. 'You saw it yourself.' I shut my eyes tight, pressed my lips together, but I couldn't hold it back. 'Dead, dead, dead,' Mum sobbed.

A fist forced its way up through my throat. It was like drowning from the inside. All I could do was scream.

That it was my ball.

That before I knew, I had jumped in after it.

That I was swimming even before I remembered I wasn't allowed to.

That the ball kept floating off ahead of me. That I turned and waved to Dad on the beach and shouted that it was okay for me to swim here after all, that I could swim really well, that it felt like I was whizzing down a slide.

His face. Red. Furious. And suddenly he was right behind me. I called to him not to be angry with me, that I was going to get my ball back, and just look how well I was swimming. I tried to paddle closer to him, and it was then I felt the sea holding me back, tugging at my arms, my legs, even trying to grasp my fingers. No matter how fast I swam, I felt myself drifting further from the rocks.

Dad's hands seized me by the shoulders, turned me on my back. His breathing heavy beside my ear. Beneath me, the thrashing and churning of his legs. It seemed there was no moving forward. All the while I could only think of my ball, drifting further and further away from us. I shouted that I hadn't done it on purpose. Dad coughed and panted next to my head. Some of his strokes dragged me under for a moment. I gagged.

At last we reached the shore. He thrust me up against the rocks, his fist under my backside. I climbed up under my own steam and knew for certain now that he would hit me, belt me round both sides of my head. I made myself small, closed my eyes, clenched my hands into fists, and held my arms stiff at my sides.

But the blows didn't come.

I opened my eyes a timid fraction. I couldn't see him anywhere. Only my ball, a dot on the waves. And, closer, a pale shape just beneath the surface. A shape that must be my dad.

'Da...? Dad?'

He wasn't angry at all. He was swimming after my ball!

'Da-ad,' I cheered, though I knew he couldn't hear me underwater. 'Over there, Dad!' He wasn't mad at me, at least not all that much, cos he was off after my ball.

Any moment I expected a hand to break the surface, his head to rise, his mouth gasping for air. I'd cheer him on and point to the exact spot where my ball was floating.

Underwater, the pale shape slid further out of focus. I tried to imagine how long someone could hold his breath. In my head, I started to count. When I reached fifty, I stopped. He was still swimming, only now I couldn't see him as clearly. I had to look off to one side to make him out in the grey water. Something in my knee began to tremble. 'Dad!' I called. 'Dad!' Again I began to count.

Gulls and terns were sitting on the rocks and diving for fish. Waves continued to slosh into clefts between the rocks. A crab crawled into view. Everything was normal, except for the trickle of blood on my knee, a cut I could hardly feel. I clambered onto a higher rock. For a second I thought I saw my ball off in the distance between two waves. But then I couldn't see it anymore.

Dad was gone.

I was to blame. I was to blame.

Mum stared straight at me. Her sharp finger was up close to my face. 'If this is true... My God, if this is true. All this time you've said nothing. If this is true...'

I tried desperately to cling to her, to hide my face in the hollow beside her breast, to disappear. She knocked me away with her elbow. I fell to the floor. 'You,' she repeated, over and over. 'So it was you.' Her hand clamped my neck like a fox trap, my head snapped back.

'That's not how it was,' I groaned. 'Maybe that's not how it was.'

She squeezed even harder. I could feel her nails digging into my neck. 'So this is all your fault.' Her words were razor sharp. I closed my eyes. I would let her hit me, lashing out as much as she wanted, slapping my head, my back, my hands. I wouldn't make a sound.

Instead, she locked me in my room.

One day.

Then another.

I slept propped up on the corner of my bed, too scared to knock on my door or to call out that I was hungry. I slurped water from the tap of my washbasin and crept back under the covers. Once, I turned the tap on full and stared at the streaming water till it made me cry. Guilt gnawed my stomach hollow.

It wasn't till the second morning that I heard fumbling at the lock. I pretended to be asleep but peeked out through half-closed eyes. The handle didn't move. When I was sure Mum had gone downstairs, I tiptoed over to the door. It opened. As quietly as I could, I moved through the house.

I took some crackers from an open packet in the hall cupboard and crept back to my room.

I wanted her to lock me up again.

20

She never called Dad 'Dad' again, only Birk. Her Birk, so I would know the blame was mine and the sorrow hers. We came no closer than opposite sides of the table.

Dad never fell out of the tap again.

We stopped tearing the pages off the calendar the day Dad disappeared. After a few months, Mum took it down off the nail and tossed it into the stove. The fire almost choked on its own smoke. Nothing much changed. Mum kept making soup for three. When the winter wind howled through the house, we cut up old socks and used a screwdriver to push the strips as deep into the cracks as we could, cracks that grew wider each year. In spring, Mum dug over the vegetable garden and seeded the beds. By summer they were overrun with weeds, and we ate tinned veg.

Everything that had belonged to Dad stayed in its familiar place. With a tea towel for a blindfold, he would have been able to walk through the hall, into the living room, take three Dad-sized paces across the rug, and fall backward: his easy chair was there to catch him. Without even looking, he'd be able to switch on the lamp and reach for his newspapers on the side table. Mum would bring him his coffee, and meanwhile I'd hear the pages rustle as he pulled out the finance section so I could use it to light the fire.

Mum got good at saying nothing. I already was. If her silence lasted too long, it helped if I went looking for a present to give her.

Sometimes I came home with a grazed elbow for her to patch up. That helped, too, though I couldn't do it all that often. Taking a strip of sticking plaster, a pair of scissors, and a bottle of iodine from the drawer, she'd part her legs and beckon me over to stand between them. She'd take hold of my wrist and twist my arm to get a better look at the wound. Wincing, she'd ask if it hurt. I always said it wasn't that bad. As she screwed the top off the iodine bottle, she'd warn me it was going to sting. Then I'd feel her breath blow gently on the wound. 'You have good blood,' she'd say. 'Look after it.'

My days with Mum ended up being so alike, I can barely remember anything about them. Little by little, Dad faded into photographs. Without wanting to, without even realizing, it was something I got used to.

Karl regularly invited me to go over to Tramsund with him, but I couldn't leave Mum all by herself. It was as if she had lost a leg but still insisted on trying to walk. So I became her other leg. When I plucked up the courage to ask her about going to Tramsund, all she said was 'Oh.'

I told Karl I was allowed to go, and it was only then that I realized how much I wanted to. The morning before we were due to leave, Mum lay curled up in bed, moaning, the covers pulled over her head. She squeaked when she breathed. I brought her a glass of water and some aspirin. 'You go now,' she said in a voice so feeble I decided to stay.

Another time, she needed my help to dig over the vegetable garden. 'You're not going to let your mother do all this work on her own, are you?' she asked, squeezing my arm. As soon as Karl had taken the boat out, she made me an omelette.

One morning I came down to find her in the kitchen with her coat on, rummaging in a drawer for her passport and purse. Her legs were the colour of tan stockings, her feet crammed into high-heeled shoes. 'What are you doing?'

'I'll be back this evening.'

'Are you going to Tramsund?'

'Your Mum's off to the dentist.'

'Can I come, too?'

'But then there would be no one here.' She cupped her hands around my cheeks. 'Someone always has to stay on the island. To wait.'

'And you want me to do that?'

'Please.'

'But you'll be all alone.'

'Karl's taking me.'

In no time at all, Karl was helping Mum over the rail of his boat, her coat flapping in the breeze. I looked down at her from my bedroom window. She didn't see me wave.

It was a day of secret pleasures. I sneaked into Karl's living room to watch TV and lay in Mum's bed. Now and then I buried my face in Dad's jumpers and breathed in their smell.

In the years that followed, she went off with Karl a few more times, twice to go to the dentist or the doctor and once to arrange something to do with Dad; she wouldn't say what. I never went off on Karl's boat.

Ten. Eleven. Twelve. My birthdays passed unnoticed. We didn't celebrate anything, not even Christmas. Karl usually invited us over on New Year's Eve. Mum would accept, but when the evening arrived and he knocked on the door, we'd be tucked up in our beds with the lights out. Every spring and autumn, Mum would cut Karl's hair.

In the garden, the trees and bushes grew taller and fought for space. They hemmed in the house as the years passed and made it seem smaller. Eventually we had to turn on the lights in the daytime.

I grew taller, too. I only noticed when I first saw a bare patch of torn pink skin on top of Mum's head. I wanted to ask how she got it, but I didn't dare. I felt like I'd seen it without her permission.

Taking a bath, I discovered a dark curl of hair growing under my balls. The longer I looked at it, the less I was able to imagine it hadn't always been there. Up in my bedroom I snipped it off with the scissors on my Swiss Army knife.

In two weeks it had grown back.

Looking in Dad's wardrobe gave me a kind of hope. His jumpers, shirts, and trousers lay there patiently, reassuringly. It was the same with his books, the tools that lay untouched in the shed, and his boots under the hat stand. We'd blow the dust off once in a while and Mum sometimes ran a cloth over them. That was all.

One day a glossy boarding-school brochure appeared on the table. The cover showed smiling boys posing with their arms around one another's shoulders, or chasing after a football, or poring over books in a room full of bunk beds. I tried not to pay it any attention but there it was, day after day, shining up at me. I knew Mum had read it. The village with the school was nowhere to be found in my atlas. The brochure said it was a complex far from distractions and protected by a forest. I had to look up 'distractions' in the dictionary. After I read it, I put the brochure back exactly as I'd found it, but Mum could still tell I'd had a look.

'Have you seen this one?' She showed me a photo of some boys chopping wood. 'That's what boys your age get up to.'

I stared at the supper on my plate.

The brochure wound up on a chair, then on a pile of post, and eventually seemed to disappear.

A few weeks later, as we were washing up, I cautiously mentioned that Karl had asked me to go to Tramsund with him again and that I really wanted to go. She seemed not to hear, so I asked her again. She pulled the plug and dried her hands on the tea towel I was holding. I said it would only be for a day.

Later that evening I came back from the toilet to find her sitting at the window, flicking through the school brochure. The pages were curled at the corners. 'Look,' she said, pointing at one of the photos. 'That boy's writing a letter.'

'Looks to me like he's doing his homework.'

'Is that what you think?'

'There are books on the table and he has a ruler in his hand.'

'Ah, but you can tell he hasn't been home for a long time,' Mum went on. 'I think he's writing a letter.'

She'd never send me there. I knew that. It would mean being here all by herself, and that would be even worse than being here with me. Still, I never asked her about Tramsund again.

Year in, year out, bulky envelopes full of tests kept arriving. The textbooks became thicker, with fewer drawings and smaller print. They made me feel lost and bewildered. Mostly I would sit at the kitchen table so Mum could see me studying. Whenever she walked past, I'd scribble away in my notebook and frown intently as I flipped between random pages. When I showed her what I'd been doing, she'd only say, 'That's an awful lot of numbers.'

I was afraid to open the envelopes that contained my test results. They disappeared into the fire. Before long, new tests arrived with even more questions I didn't understand.

I decided to write a letter to ask the dear sirs or madams if they would kindly remove Mikael Hammermann from their files because he had become deceased a few months ago, and the post they sent was a confrontation with our tragic loss. I'd found the word 'confrontation' in the dictionary. It made the whole thing sound a bit more serious. 'Tragic' seemed like a good word, too. I swirled Mum's signature at the bottom and scribbled the date next to it. Then I started all over again. The mother of a deceased son would never have such a swirly signature, and 'deceased' sounded a bit too dead. In the new letter, I added an urgent request to leave us in peace due to our grief. I couldn't come up with another word for 'deceased', so I wrote it the second time as well, ending with a sadder version of Mum's signature.

I stuffed the letter into the return envelope along with the empty test sheets and licked it shut. I sellotaped over the flap and punched a couple of staples through it for good measure. I kept the envelope under my mattress.

The morning the groceries arrived, Mum produced the pouch for our post and put it in one of the crates.

'Wait!' I shouted. 'My tests!' I ran up to my room to fetch the envelope.

Mum wanted to take it off me, but I snatched the pouch from her hands and put it in myself. 'My clever boy,' she said, stroking my cheek. 'You're not one to give up.' For a few seconds everything felt light and full of air. Outside, Brigitta gave three blasts on his horn.

'Off you go, quick,' Mum said.

Two weeks after he'd told us Dad was down wi' the eels, the grocery man didn't turn up. But after another two weeks, our crates of groceries appeared on the quay. That became his new routine, and it became my job to arrange everything with him. Mum wrote the lists. It turned out Dad had eaten as much as Mum and I put together, all those years. We ordered half of everything, except for kitchen roll. We seemed to get through much more of that.

As soon as I handed Brigitta the pouch, he sailed straight out of the bay. There went my stupid letter. I felt a sudden pang that gnawed at my stomach for days. How could I have been such an idiot? Now Mum would never be able to stroke my cheek again and tell me I wasn't a giver-upper. It's not like I could send another letter saying, 'Sorry, my mistake! My son's alive after all.'

I hoped they would somehow overlook my letter. Perhaps they wouldn't believe it, or they'd just send their condolences and then I could write back and say there must be some misunderstanding, that my heart went out to the parents of that other boy called Mikael Hammermann, but my son was alive and well. That's what I'd do. Then Mum could go on telling me I wasn't one to give up when I waved the test-sheet envelope at her.

The next time the post arrived, I tried to look through the envelopes while I was still outside on the quay, but Mum was standing at the kitchen window with her arms crossed, staring at me. I left the pouch unopened and carried the grocery crates inside. Her name would be on the envelope, of course, or it would say *To the parents of Mikael Hammermann*, so I'd have to swipe it before she noticed and sneak it up to my room.

The back of my throat tingled anxiously as Mum picked up the pouch. Bank statements, a chequebook, and some bills were all it contained. Two weeks later there was no reply, either. In the hope that she wouldn't suspect anything, I spent hours at the kitchen table, browsing aimlessly through my textbooks and filling up my notebooks.

Not long after, I tore a page off the calendar at the end of the day and discovered I had turned fifteen.

1

When I was little, I always thought the skin of your nipples would get darker and tougher as you got older. I've been fifteen for a while now, and my nipples are darker but they still feel tender. A bit like a bruise in an apple.

Steam stopped rising from the bathwater ages ago. I wrap the chain around my toes, pull the plug, and a whirlpool appears between my feet. My willy and the hair around it move in slow motion underwater. It's nice to lie in the bath till all the water has drained away and slowly feel the weight return to my body.

With my chin tucked against my chest, I look at the ring of eight hairs around my nipple. A sad little sun. I pinch a hair between my nails and pull gently. It looks like a needle is trying to force its way up through my skin from the inside. The last of the water gurgles and is gone. My willy has got a bit stiffer.

I dry myself roughly with a scratchy towel, pull on my clothes, and open the top window just enough to let the damp air escape.

2

'Are you dead?'

'What do you mean?'

Mum is standing with her back to me, holding a letter. I can see the Education Department logo in the top right corner. 'Is that what the letter says?' I ask, sounding as surprised as possible. A torn envelope is lying on the table. Stupid of me not to notice it in the post.

'It says here they've received a letter from me. "We regret to inform you that this is a rather irregular way to report a death, and feel obliged to point out that such matters must first be reported to the authorities... It goes without saying that we will stop sending test modules and textbooks until such time as a report has been made. We would like to extend our deepest sympathies for your tragic loss."' Mum's hair is flat and tangled where she's slept on it. 'Did you do this behind my back?'

My chin trembles slightly. ''Course not.'

'So what makes them think you're dead?'

'Maybe it's a mistake.'

'You think so?'

'Can I have a read?'

'Mikael?'

'Yes.'

'You're lying.' She turns to face me. 'I can tell.'

'I'm not,' I blurt out.

She takes a step toward me. Her legs are bare and white, her dressing gown is hanging open like a curtain. 'Why did you do this?'

'I didn't.'

She pokes my chest with her finger as if she wants to leave a dent. 'You're lying.'

'It was an accident.'

'You accidentally wrote to tell them you're dead.'

'I wanted them to stop sending me those tests.'

'And *this* is what you came up with?'

'They kept on sending me tests and more books. I couldn't understand them anymore. And then this happened.'

'When?'

'A month ago, maybe longer.'

'All by yourself, without a word to me...'

'Yes.'

'So you think you can do without me.'

'What? 'Course not.'

'The mighty Mikael Hammermann thinks he can handle things all by himself.'

'That's not true. That's not what I want. Honest, I don't. Can't you write back and tell them it's all my fault? That it's not what we want?'

Calmly, Mum tears the letter in half. 'If you go sneaking around behind my back, you're going to have to face the consequences.'

'I'm sorry. It's not what I want, honest.'

'There's no going back now.' The grate of the stove squeaks open. Orange coals glow brighter, flakes of ash whirl into the kitchen. The letter begins to smoke and blacken, then goes up in flames. 'You will keep no secrets from me.'

I look at the floor, at her feet, which are nearly as white as the tiles. She hasn't cut her toenails in a long time.

There's a knock at the door.

I hesitate, unsure whether to open it. Mum pulls the cord of her dressing gown tight around her waist and turns the key in the lock. Karl begins to talk as soon as the door opens. 'My, my. Locking the door these days?

Not for fear of the neighbours, I hope.' He leans an elbow against the doorpost. 'Still in your dressing gown. That's the life, eh.'

'To what do we owe the pleasure?' Mum asks.

'Huh?'

'Why did you knock?'

'No reason. We haven't seen each other in a while, so I reckoned it was high time I paid the girl next door a visit.' Karl grins. 'Any news?'

'None since last time you asked.'

'Fine,' says Karl. The wind is sucking at the door and Mum has to hold it open with her foot. Karl peers over her shoulder. 'Good afternoon, matey.'

I raise my hand.

'Your boy's been helping me out lately.'

'So I've seen.'

'I thought you'd appreciate me giving him a bit of work now and then.'

'Can't say as I do.'

'He's a good help. Sorts the fish, guts and scales 'em. Sweeps up a bit, of course. Just the ticket for a young lad. Showing him the ropes, bit by bit. We'll make a fisherman of him yet.'

'I wouldn't if I were you.'

'What d'you mean?'

'I wouldn't go to any trouble.'

'How come?'

'My son's not one for sticking at things.'

'Well, it's not like he has to become a fisherman straight off. For now he's a good help. And learning a thing or two from me's not going to do him any harm, now, is it?' Karl makes a show of yawning and stretching.

Flies are buzzing in angular circuits around the kitchen light. They're already slowing down. More flies crawl groggily over the windowsill and up the windowpane. They've flown into the glass so often, their tiny brains are damaged. All that's left for them to do is die. Winter will have come and gone before new ones start circling through the kitchen again. When I was younger, I'd catch one in my fist and shake it as hard as I could. The old ones were easiest. They'd sit there on my palm for a minute or two, as if they'd been drugged. I was Mum's lion tamer, only with flies instead of lions.

'The nights are already drawing in,' says Karl. 'Maybe we could see more of each other in the evenings?'

'Why?'

'I mean, uh… where does it say we have to drink our coffee all by ourselves?'

'Nowhere.'

'A bit of company wouldn't do us any harm, eh? Two people alone on an island.'

'What about me?' I pipe up.

'And Mikael makes three,' says Karl.

'Mind if I shut the door?' says Mum. 'I'm catching cold.'

'Okey-doke,' says Karl and raps his knuckles on the doorpost, as if for luck. 'If you need anything, you know where to find me.' He's laughing at himself so much, it's hard to make out the words. Mum's lips tighten, and two testy little creases appear on her cheeks. 'Up to you,' chuckles Karl.

Once she's locked the back door, Mum sets a bowl and a carton of long-life milk down on the table. She sits down, scrapes her chair closer, and reaches for the box of porridge oats.

I'm still standing in the doorway.

Before she eats her porridge, Mum always waits till the milk has soaked in and it's turned into a bowl of chewed-up rope. While she's waiting, she flicks through a magazine. I want to say I'm sorry, and that I don't want to be a fisherman, but I keep my mouth shut.

I get a bowl and sit down opposite her. The carton of milk is almost empty. I give it a shake and slurp out the little that's left. I drag myself over to the cupboard under the stairs to fetch a new carton, cut a miserly mouth in the side, and fill my bowl. The powdery porridge in the box looks like sawdust. I sprinkle some into the milk and wait till it's stopped being sawdust but is nowhere near becoming chewed-up rope, and spoon it quickly into my mouth.

When I've finished I let the spoon seesaw between my fingers and tap the edge of the table. I know she hates it when I drag my feet, slurp milk from the carton, snip too small an opening in the side, and tap my spoon. She goes on steadily digging shallow holes in her grey porridge till I can't take it anymore.

I grab my raincoat from the chair and pull on my boots.

3

A curtain is trying to flap off through a broken upstairs window. The slates that still cling to the roof are white with gull shit. Birch trees drill their twigs between the boards and thrust their roots deeper into Miss Augusta's house in an effort to force it apart, one millimetre at a time. Now that part of the roof has caved in, the gulls not only line up along the gutter and the windowsills, but have also occupied the ribcage of attic beams and colonized the rooms.

I throw a stone, aiming for the highest point of the roof. It bounces off a few slates and clatters into the gaping hole of the attic. Some of the gulls spread their wings in fright, then fold them over their backs like napkins. As I approach the house, one bird cries and sets off another that sets off another. I know they wouldn't dare attack me, but just to be sure, I always have a stone clenched in my fist.

Damp has stained the wallpaper brown in the rooms under the collapsed roof, and the floorboards are forcing one another up like ice along the shore. In the hall, the door to the meter cupboard is hanging open. The wood inside is dark and mouldy and the switches are so rusty they break off when you try to flick them. Bright-green ferns push their curled leaves up through the skirting boards. The toilet bowl is missing, transplanted to our bathroom years ago.

Two gulls are sitting on the mantelpiece in the living room. They take turns screeching, exposing the red of their throats. I clap my hands. They fall silent for a moment and pick at the marble of the mantelpiece till they've settled down.

I step into the kitchen, the only place in the house that looks like it used to. There are hardly any leaks, and it's free of gull shit cos the stupid birds are too scared to pass through the bead curtain hanging in the doorway. With the kitchen cupboards closed, you don't even miss all the things I've given away as presents. There are still two plates drying on the rack by the sink. The chairs around the table wait patiently. A withered dishcloth hangs over the tap, and a polished pebble of soap lies in its dish.

Sometimes I get three mugs from one of the cupboards and put them on the table, along with the coffee pot. If I sit here for a while, it's as if Miss Augusta has just toddled into the living room to fetch something and Dad was bursting for a pee and has just nipped to the toilet. And I'm just sitting here looking out the window.

The first time I entered the house after Dad disappeared, I was too afraid to move. I stood at the front door and shouted, 'Miss Augusta? Are you there?' Only the gulls answered.

I sat down on the wooden bench, as close to the door as possible, my hands clutching my thighs. That way, if the dead Miss Augusta came into the room with a full pot of coffee in her shaky hands, she wouldn't be able to catch me doing anything. It would be like a normal visit, and at most she'd be surprised that she'd forgotten I was there. I'd jump up and tell her I was going to the kitchen to fetch myself a mug. Of course, I wouldn't have gone into the kitchen—I'd have escaped into the garden and run back to our house, screaming at the top of my lungs that she wasn't dead after all.

A framed photograph was lying face down on a table next to the bench I was sitting on. I didn't have the nerve to stand it upright. On the back was a gold sticker with the name of the photographer, A.J. Bergman of Tramsund. It was only after a storm, when some volumes of Miss Augusta's encyclopaedia fell off the bookshelf and were still lying in the same place weeks later, that I knew for certain she wasn't here anymore.

I picked up the toppled frame from the side table. Miss Augusta was unrecognizable in the black-and-white photo, but I knew it was her cos she'd told me once. Miss Augusta's parents were standing behind her and her mother had one hand resting on the shoulder of her daughter's white dress. The trees that now cast shadows in the dark house were still just sticks that reached no higher than her parents' hips. The photo was taken on the day they came to live here.

'That was a long time ago, my boy,' Miss Augusta sniffed. I could smell coffee on her breath. I parted my lips, just a little so she wouldn't notice, and tried to breathe through my mouth so I wouldn't have to smell it anymore. 'My father's long since dead, my mother, too. This photograph is all I have left of them. Apart from my things. And this.' She tapped the side of her head with a crooked finger. 'My memories.'

It was creepy to have her face so close to mine. I could see little black dots on her nose, and the bags under her eyes could've passed for earlobes.

'Can I have another biscuit?' I asked, squirming out from under her arm.

'Your life hasn't even begun.' Miss Augusta rubbed the frame on her skirt to wipe her greasy fingerprints off the glass. 'Do you know who that girl is?' she asked with a smile. 'That's me.'

Quick as I could, I snatched two biscuits from the plate. They were soft and it was easy to stuff them both into my mouth at once without spraying crumbs. I hoped Dad would hurry up with his repairs. He was up a ladder in front of the window, hammering new boards to the front of the house. We could only see his legs. Mum always said, 'That lonely old biddy breaks things on purpose just so you'll come over and fix them.'

'Oh, leave her be,' Dad replied. 'At least there's one person round here who's happy to see me.'

I was allowed to come with him when something needed repairing. 'I'll fix anything in exchange for a cup of coffee, Pernille,' he'd say with a smile.

'That's the least I can do, Birk.' And she'd wobble straight off to the kitchen to boil the water.

Dad would wink at me, light a cigarette, and start sizing up the job at hand.

The frame that held the black-and-white photo was one of the first presents I gave Mum after Dad disappeared. First I picked off the A.J. Bergman sticker and then rubbed the back of the frame with spit till I'd got rid of the last traces of glue. On the way home, I took the photo of Miss Augusta and her parents from behind the glass and let it blow out of my hand.

Mum took the frame from me, put her hand against my neck, and briefly ran her thumb up and down my throat. Then she went upstairs and slid an old portrait photo of Dad into the frame. She let me fetch the hammer from the shed and bang a nail into the wall in the hall. Dad was seventeen in the photo; it was from before they met. When I stand in front of it now, it becomes a mirror. Especially when I tilt my head slightly to one side and imitate his half smile. Even back then, Dad smoked so much that when he didn't have a cigarette between his lips, there was still space for one at the corner of his mouth. I only pose in front of the photo when I'm sure Mum won't catch me doing it.

By now I've given her so many presents, it's getting more and more difficult to find one she might like.

I look at the plates in the kitchen cupboard, the sieve, the coffee grinder, and the biscuit tin. Today I have to give her something she can use to make herself look pretty. The cutlery drawer rattles like a toolbox and I have to bash it a few times before it will open. From the

jumble inside I pick up a corkscrew and let it fall immediately; we've already got two of those. I find a pack of
five cigarettes in the drawer, tap it against my hand till
one slides out, and put it between my lips. It feels good
to walk around with the unlit cigarette dangling from
my mouth, like finding something to do with your
hands when you're feeling shy.

I climb the stairs, go into the bathroom, and look at
myself in the mirror. I turn my head slightly and hold a
lighted match to the cigarette. My chest heaves. I inhale
a few times, not too deep, and blow out the smoke. My
throat prickles as if I've breathed in sand. I try to hold
back the cough, but that only makes it worse.

I toss what's left of the cigarette into the bathtub. A
lightning-bolt crack has sliced the tiled wall. In the cupboard under the washbasin I find nail clippers and a bottle of eau de cologne. With my thumb, I dust off the
greasy neck of the bottle; it's still over half full. I slip it
into my coat pocket along with the clippers.

The landing creaks. I skirt around the rotten floorboards.
Before heading back downstairs, I decide to take a look
in the bedroom. I push open the door, and the screech of
a gull makes me jump back. She's made her nest on the
middle of the bed. Her wings flap open to scare me off,
but she's not about to abandon her eggs.

It annoys me that a stupid bird thinks this room is
hers now, just cos she happened to make her nest here. I
kick the bed and my arms tingle with the urge to lash
out at her. I grab a chair, feel its weight in my hands, and
swing it through the air in slow motion before placing it
in the doorway and sitting down.

The nest is made of scraps of curtain, reeds, twigs, and material from a blouse, shreds of which are scattered around the room. The bed is more or less the way Miss Augusta left it before she fell down the stairs, and the nest is balanced between the pillow and the downturned bedclothes. Perhaps she'd just gone down to make herself a cup of tea, and had been planning to take it back up to bed with her.

The gull shrieks like an alarm. She picks at the reeds in her nest for food that isn't there, and shifts restlessly to and fro. I am a chemical pumping through her veins: danger, danger, danger. I cross my arms and hook my ankles around the legs of the chair. I keep perfectly still, only my eyes flicker. My breathing is becoming calmer. The gull cranes her neck forward with every cry, as if she's showing me the door.

Not long after Dad disappeared, I discovered how to fade away, how to be around Mum without her noticing I was there anymore.

The sun lights a path across the room. The magazines that litter the floor wouldn't make any kind of present: wrinkled and swollen with damp, the puzzles have all been solved in Miss Augusta's shaky handwriting. I swallow. The gull doesn't notice. For her, my breathing is beginning to merge with the wind. I'm becoming part of the chair, the wardrobe, the open door, the walls. Part of everything that isn't moving. The gull turns her watchful head and opens her beak, but she's no longer able to see what she's afraid of. She moves around and her cries become softer, as if she's talking to herself. She lowers her beak and nudges the eggs underneath her. I am slowly fading from her blood.

The gull settles on her nest, then startles herself with

an unexpected squawk, as if she's woken with a jolt after falling asleep too quickly. Blurred shapes slowly flicker and melt in front of her eyes as she roots around among her feathers.

I am invisible.

She does not make a sound.

4

'For you.'

I press the nail clippers into Mum's palm. She gives me a curt nod.

'And this, too.' I produce the eau de cologne from my coat pocket. 'Open it.'

'I can smell something.'

'It's perfume.'

'You smell of something.'

'Me?'

'It's on your breath.'

I clamp my lips together.

'Here, let me smell.' Her nose is almost touching mine. I can see the frayed threads of her irises. 'Please?'

Hesitantly, I open my mouth, just a little. She moves even closer and sniffs a few times.

'Mmm,' she says. 'Nice.'

I part my lips a little more.

'Have you been smoking?'

'No.'

'Then what's that smell?'

'It was only half a cigarette.'

'I knew it.'

'I just wanted to give it a try.'

'Where did you get it?'

'I found some at Miss Augusta's.'

She smiles.

'I liked it,' I stammer.

'That's my boy.' She runs a hand lightly through my hair.

5

'Well, if it isn't Young Master Hammermann, back at last.' When Karl calls me that, it's never a good sign. 'Fine time to come and help. I'm just finishing up for the day.'

'Sorry.'

'Mother always knows best.'

'How d'you mean?'

'She said you weren't one for sticking at things. Looks like you proved her right again.'

'I said I was sorry.'

'I can get along just fine without your help. Saves me money. Fish, too, come to that.'

To convince him he still needs me, I grab the brush and get busy sweeping the seaweed and other crap over toward the edge of the quay. A little fish appears from under the brown fronds and strands.

'You missed one.'

I pick it up and toss it into one of the containers.

'Wrong container,' Karl grunts. 'That's smelt.'

'Where does it go, then?'

'Big help you are.'

'I was busy.'

'Oh, Young Master Hammermann was busy,' sniggers Karl. 'And what, pray tell, is keeping you so busy around here?'

I keep on brushing stubbornly. 'Things.'

'What kind of things?'

'Mum.'

'Your mother?'

'I have to do stuff for her.'

Karl sighs. 'Hmm, she's a tough one all right, that mother of yours. But when all's said and done, she's still a woman making do on her own.'

'She's *not* on her own.'

Karl gawps at me, jaw slack, teeth like a row of lopsided tombstones. 'Is there someone else?'

'Me.'

'You?'

'Yes.'

There's a kind of relief in his chuckle. 'Isn't it time you went and feasted your eyes on the lassies? Over yonder.' He points over his shoulder toward the horizon. 'Ladyville.'

Till last year, I thought he was talking about a real town called Ladyville, but then I looked it up in my atlas and it turns out it doesn't even exist. On another map I discovered a little island called Papa—best name ever for a desert island. When Karl said Ladyville he just meant Tramsund, a dot on the map that looks like it's a big deal but only cos there's not another town for miles. Dad and I went there together a couple of times, and I remember flashes of those trips. The main thing I remember is getting on a bus with only two empty seats left, one behind the other. Dad sat on the seat in front of me and craned his neck restlessly every time we turned a corner, to make sure we didn't miss our stop. His hand kept snaking back between the seats to feel if my knee was still there. The same hand clamped my wrist tightly as we walked past the buildings. There were people everywhere. I remember all the different types of biscuits in the supermarket, too, and the dentist I couldn't really understand even though he was speaking the same language as us. He kept saying I had too many cavities for a boy my age, and I remember having to open my mouth so wide I thought it would rip at the corners. The dentist had hair growing out of his ears.

I remember all the clothes Dad didn't buy me, and gazing back at the town for a long, long time from the deck at the back of the boat as we sailed home. Dad was in the cabin with Karl, smoking. When we got home, Mum said, 'Well, it'll be a while before you need to go over *there* again.'

'Ladyville.' Karl's getting carried away. 'That's where you'll find 'em. Big. Small. One-legged. Some smell of fish, some of chicken soup.'

'What kind do you have?'

'Huh?'

'What kind?'

His laugh sounds thick and greasy. 'I eat whatever's on special.' Karl's laugh nosedives into a rasping cough. He bends over and tries to thump himself on the back.

'Leave it to me.' I whack him a couple of times between the shoulder blades.

'That'll do,' he says with tears in his eyes. 'Forgot my medicine.' He pulls a crumpled pouch of tobacco from his trouser pocket. 'Forty a day keeps the doctor away.' I've heard that line a hundred times, but I chuckle anyway cos I'm glad he's stopped thinking about how little help I've been.

'That's more like it,' says Karl, and gives another cough or two.

'Can I have one, too?'

'A cigarette?'

'Uh-huh.'

'What'll your mother say?'

'She doesn't mind.'

'Is that right?'

'But I don't know how to roll my own, yet.'

'If you end up in trouble when you get home, it's your lookout. And if she comes over to give me a hard time, I'm playing dumb.'

I shrug my shoulders.

'Okay then,' he says. 'Here's how you do it.' Karl takes a pinch of tobacco and uses a finger from each hand to spread it along the cigarette paper.

'Then you have to lick it.' He looks up at me as he moistens the paper with his limp pink tongue. 'Nothing to it, eh? You could train a seal to do it.' He hands me the cigarette.

'I'd rather do my own.'

'Young Master H. is full of demands today,' he says, but hands me the tobacco anyway. 'Don't go wasting it all.'

I concentrate hard and do my best to roll a tight tube. It ends up being all weedy and crooked, with tobacco spilling out of both ends.

'Not bad for a first go,' says Karl, slapping his coat pockets.

'Lighter's over there.' I point to the low wall.

Karl holds the flame up to my cigarette, but I take the lighter out of his hand so I can light it myself.

On my own I had no trouble taking a drag without coughing, but with Karl here it's a different story. I blow more than I suck but at least I manage to generate a lot of smoke. It's a good feeling, standing here by the wall beside Karl. Gazing at our house, I notice I've forgotten to switch off my bedroom light. Stupid.

Our house is small when you look at it from a distance. The cheapest house in the world, Dad used to call it. When he started on about that, he always ended up talking about his parents. 'They set out the path I was supposed to follow, but they kept getting lost themselves. The only good thing I got from them was enough of an inheritance to live out the rest of my days as a poor man.' He put his hand on my neck and squeezed a little too hard. 'If we watch the pennies, there may even be enough left for you. Then you'll not have to do anything you don't want to do for the rest of your life.' That's why he'd bought the cheapest house in the world, and why we lived the cheapest life.

I try to suck some smoke into my mouth so I have something to blow out. I manage it twice, but the third time I break into a cough.

'Take it easy, lad.'

'I am.' My voice wobbles.

'Isn't it about time you took a little trip with me?'

'To Tramsund?'

'Just for the day. Over to the fish market and back. You can help me unload and make up for a few of those times you didn't turn up.'

'Maybe.' Now the light in my room is off, and I wonder whether it was on in the first place.

'I've got to go,' I say.

'Already?'

'Forgot something.'

'You haven't even finished your cigarette.'

'When will you need me again?'

'Day after tomorrow, I think. Maybe the day after that.'

I hold out my hand.

'For picking up a brush?' He slaps my outstretched palm. 'Forget it, Hammermann. Not a penny.'

Up in my room, everything's exactly the way I left it. No fresh towels under my washbasin. Maybe she just came in to switch the light off. I can hear roars of laughter downstairs, coming from the radio in her bedroom. I press my ear to the floor but I can't make out what she's listening to.

6

It's only when I wake up the next morning that I notice I forgot to close the curtains. The sky is already clear blue, though it's still holding a pale moon. Nothing else to see but a few white criss-cross trails left by planes.

I prop myself up against the pillow and slide the covers down. My cock curves up toward my belly button. I push it away with my palm, but that only makes it stiffer. It used to go soft when I squeezed it, bent it, or tugged hard on my foreskin. When I do that now it only demands more attention. My nipples turn hard and nubby. I tiptoe over to the washbasin, the stick between my legs swaying clumsily with every step. I close my eyes so I don't have to look at myself in the mirror.

The warmth of my cock tingles in my fist. The skin is soft. Red flecks, stripes, flashes of white quiver inside my eyelids.

My balls tap faster and faster against the cold rim of the washbasin. I feel a gentle cramp, like I've been holding in my piss for too long, only deeper. I grit my teeth.

A flash.

White.

A chill hits the back of my neck.

Feeling sheepish as usual, I rinse away the gobs of white. They remind me of the rubbery threads that leak from the cracks in an egg and drift around in the boiling water. My spunk disappears down the plug hole, and just to be sure I wipe the basin clean with a corner of my towel. Not wanting to look at my shrinking erection, I pull on my underpants in a hurry. I spray deodorant around the room till it makes me cough and then squirt some under my arms. I hold a rough flannel under the tap and give my face a quick wipe. Then I brush my teeth. When I spit, the white foam is speckled pink with blood.

Thankfully I feel my cock returning to normal, though it's still warm. A shiny droplet has welled up in the opening and left a thin snail trail on the inside of my pants. I wipe it off, turn on the washbasin tap again, and piss the water yellow.

Mum is sitting at the table with her bowl of porridge. I go over to the cupboard and get a bowl for myself. There's a sparkle of sorts in her eyes. 'Good morning.'

'You too,' I reply.

She chuckles.

'What's up?'

'Nothing,' she says airily. 'Nothing at all.'

I start to feel uncomfortable. She stares intently at her bowl and her chuckle becomes a giggle.

'What's the matter? Tell me.'

She tries to stifle her laughter, but one more look at me and a cackle fills the kitchen. Her eyes are shining with tears. 'Wha-hadda we have here?' she howls.

'What *is* it?' I ask.

She points to my face. 'Yagorratash.'

Can she *tell* I've just had a wank? 'I can't understand what you're saying.'

'Yuvgorratashcummin.'

'A what?'

'A mooooose-tache.' She leans back in her chair and appears to be all laughed out. 'A big fat teenage caterpillar.'

Dumfounded, I slap my hand over my mouth.

'Nothing to be ashamed of.'

I get up to fill the kettle. With my back to her I run my fingers along my lip. It feels soft, nothing more.

'That 'tache has got to go,' she says. 'Or you'll end up like a cactus.'

'It doesn't bother me.'

'Bother you? No, 'course not.'

'Well then?'

'I'm the one who has to look at it all day long. So if it's all the same to you, it can go.'

I hand her a cup of coffee and our fingers touch for a moment. I want to put it down on the table in front of her, but she takes it straight from my hand. 'You're becoming a man, Mikael. Whether you want to or not.'

I drink my coffee down in big hot gulps.

7

Miss Augusta's bathroom mirror isn't flat like ours. If I get too close it makes my nose look big and daft. When I run my fingertips over the faint dark fuzz on my upper lip, it doesn't seem to exist. But my tongue knows it's there. The hairs are still much too short to cut with the kitchen scissors. The longer I run my tongue over my lip, the stranger it feels. It's like the hairs have been glued on.

The gull treats me to the same welcome as last time. I sit down on the chair and put my feet up on the bed. It's one of those leather chairs that look like they're covered in belly buttons. I prise one loose. The gull squawks like a squeaky hinge and I toss her the button. She snatches it out of the air, holds it in her beak for a second or two, then spits it out again.

It's too late in the season for her to be on the nest. She's probably sitting on eggs that will never hatch. Some gulls keep that up for weeks on end. While all the other nests are empty and cheeping chicks are tottering over rocks and under bushes, they go on brooding, desperately defending their fortress of straw and twigs. Some even stick it out till the frost arrives and forces them off the nest. By that time most of the hatched chicks can already fly pretty well. The starving nest-sitters pounce on any leftover scraps of fish and are lost in a screeching swarm. Their abandoned eggs freeze within minutes and fall prey to rats. Either that, or they're pecked empty by other gulls.

Once, I drove a gull from her nest with a stick and snatched her four eggs quick as I could. I put them in a pan of water, boiled them on our cooker, and then put them back. She didn't seem to notice and went right on brooding.

Another time I even managed to scare off a gull and replace her egg with a speckled pebble I'd found on the beach. It was exactly the right shape. The gull nestled back down on her fortress while I picked open the shell of her unborn chick. It had a tiny wet body, all folded up, veins as fine as hairs, and a wobbly neck propping up a head that was way too big. Its tiny beak was the same pale pink as its thin skin, its closed eyes were like swollen mouths with dark patches under them. I tried to keep the chick warm in my hand but it died. It weighed the same dead as alive. There wasn't much weight to life. In fact, it weighed nothing at all.

I take a couple of squashed, sticky sweets from my inside pocket in an attempt to lure her off her nest. One by one I peel off the wrappers and throw her the sweets. The gull snatches at them, but they land well short at the foot of the bed. I hold my hands still, breathing quietly. The gull looks at me, then back at the sweets on the bed. Stretching her neck, she opens her beak slightly as if that will bring her closer, but then pulls back to peck randomly at the plastic and straw in her nest and rearrange the eggs beneath her. She shifts restlessly to and fro and warily raises herself up. Then, like someone charging into the cold sea with half a mind to run straight back to their towel, she lunges across the bed and greedily snaps up the sweets.

Her nest holds a single egg. One grey, speckled egg. My hands tingle. I can almost feel how warm and smooth it is, what it would feel like to crush it. When I go to grab it, the frightened gull squirts a streak of shit. Wings spread wide, she dives toward me and pecks my fingers. Her body slams into me, rough webbed feet rasp my arms and little claws scratch. I lurch backward. She pecks at my ears and even plucks a beakful of hair from my head. I manage to grab the chair and, fending her off, I tumble onto the landing.

Stamping my way through the front garden, I can still hear her screeching. I pick up a stone and throw it at the bedroom window. It leaves a little crack. 'Stupid fucking bird.'

8

For the last year or two, Brigitta has been bringing passengers with him every so often, visitors who haven't come to see us but are on their way to another island. Either that, or they're heading back to Tramsund. Sometimes he drops a group of tourists somewhere so they can catch a boat to somewhere else. They always sit on the little wooden bench outside his cabin, bunched together under the portholes in their brightly coloured rain gear and massive walking boots, looking like they're off to conquer the North Pole. 'Pays well,' says Brigitta. 'Cash in hand, no questions asked. Brings in a damn sight more than them crates o' yours.'

While Brigitta and I swap crates, the passengers climb stiffly over the rail and stride up and down the quay. They talk in loud voices and wave their cameras around, taking photos of the weirdest things: our moss-covered rain barrel, a twisted birch tree, a fishing net that Karl has hung out to dry, our rickety garden gate that won't close anymore. Now and then, one of the snazzy-anorak brigade wants me to go and stand next to something. They click the button a few times, look at their little screen, and nod contentedly. Sometimes they let me see the result, pointing at the screen and then at me like I'm some kind of moron.

Just the other week, he turned up with a bunch of people who had posh town accents. They shouted to one another about how lovely and quiet and deserted it was here. One woman pointed to the path and asked me where it took you. 'Here,' I told her.

'"Hee-yur"?' she giggled.

'I don't talk like that.'

'Oh no? D'you no tok luk thah?'

'Listen to this!' she called to the others. 'I asked him where you end up if you take this path and you'll never guess what he said... Hee-yur.' They all had a good chuckle at that.

Today Brigitta has a boy with him. I spot him even before they reach the quay.

'My son,' says Brigitta gruffly.

The boy glances at me. 'Hi.'

'Hi,' I say, though I'm not sure he can hear me.

'He's done wi' school.' Brigitta takes the empty crates off me and sends his son down to heave our full crates up on deck. 'He'll be comin' wi' me from now on.'

Brigitta takes out his lighter and relights his cigarette. 'You two can sort this out between yis, eh?' Without waiting for an answer, he steps onto the quayside. 'I've got someone to see.' Brigitta shambles up to Karl's house. Before he can knock at the door, Karl comes out and greets him with a slap on the shoulder.

Brigitta's son and I look at each other in silence. His hair is shaved to the wood and I can see his scalp through the stubble. He doesn't have a moustache like I do, but he has got some wispy black hair growing in front of his ears. I'd take that instead of the mouldy fuzz on my upper lip any day.

'D'you live here?' he asks. 'Is this like... it?'

'How d'you mean?'

'You know, this house and that house.'

'There's another house over the back.'

'So that's three.'

'Yep.'

We look at Karl and Brigitta. 'Is he your dad?' I ask for the sake of asking. Dozy, of course: his dad's just told me that himself. Luckily the boy just nods.

'Your dad's dead, eh? At least that's what mine said.'

I kick away some stones. A jellyfish drifts past underwater. 'Where do you live?'

He points out to sea. 'Tramsud.'

'You mean Tramsund?'

'Only folk that don't live there call it that.'

'I've been there before.'

'Bugger all to do. Except my girlfriend lives there. And a few friends I ride around with at night on Dad's scooter. Two more years and I'm outta there.'

'You've got a girlfriend?'

''Course I have.' A moment's silence. 'It's even more boring here.'

I feel like he's talking about me. 'It's not that bad.'

'What d'you do here all day?'

I frantically rack my brains for something that might impress him. 'I help Karl a lot. He's a fisherman and he's always going over to Tramsud.'

'So now it's Tramsud, all of a sudden?'

'I've got a house,' I go on. 'I spend a fair bit of time there. It's all mine. On the other side of the island.'

'Your own house?'

'Sort of.'

The boy cranes his neck as if he's expecting to see that far. He's wearing a thin silver chain.

'I've got a chain just like that,' I lie.

The boy nods indifferently and feels under his shirt collar.

'What kind of girlfriend do you have?'

'What *kind?*' he sniggers.

'Yeah.'

'Just a girlfriend.'

'Oh. Right.'

'What were you thinking of?'

'Dunno.'

'How many kinds d'you think there are?'

'Quite a few.'

'I'm betting you haven't got one?'

I bob my head around without committing to a yes or a no.

'Does your girlfriend live in Tramsud, too?'

'Close by.'

Brigitta shambles back toward us, stuffing a piece of paper he got from Karl into his breast pocket. 'Let's be gettin' on.' The son climbs on board behind his father.

'I'm Mikael.'

The boy snorts.

'What's so funny?'

'My girlfriend's name is Mikaella.'

Brigitta starts the engine of his boat and revs her up. The funnel pumps out black smoke that's whipped away instantly on the wind.

'What's your name, then?'

'What?'

'Your name.'

'Ingmar.' Without another glance in my direction he walks round the cabin. I look at the contents of our grocery crates. Ingmar winds a rope around his hand and his elbow. When they're almost clear of the bay, I can't resist the urge to raise my hand. Luckily, after a second or two, Ingmar waves back.

'Tramsud,' I mumble. 'Tramsud.' I want to head over to Karl's for a chat, but he's already gone inside.

9

'Who was that?'

I can hear her voice but not where it's coming from. 'Up here,' she says before I can ask. She's standing at the top of the attic stairs outside my room.

'Have you been in my room?'

'I asked you who that boy was.'

'What boy?'

'How many boys have you seen today?'

'Ingmar.'

'What did he want?'

'Nothing. He's from Tramsud.'

'Tramsud?'

'Tramsund.'

'And?'

'We just talked.'

'What about?'

'He's helping his dad. And he's got a girlfriend.'

'Is that all?'

I shrug my shoulders.

'You have a lot to say for yourself.'

'What d'you mean?'

'If you ask me, you talk a lot.'

'I hardly say a word.'

'Not to me, you don't.'

'He rides on his dad's scooter and his girlfriend's called Mikaella.'

'Why should I care about his scooter or what his girl-friend's called?'

'You asked, didn't you?'

'All I'm saying is it's odd that Mikael Hammermann won't say a word to me, but stand him next to Karl or the son of that bastard of a grocery man, and there's no shut-ting him up.'

'Sorry.'

'Only say sorry if you mean it.'

'I mean it.'

'And what are you apologizing for?'

'Because.'

'You don't mean it at all,' she says.

'I'll talk to you more, if that's what you want.'

'*You* should want to.'

'I do want to, honest.'

'Good.'

10

It's sometime during the night. I pull my feet back from the cold end of the bed and roll over. Suddenly I'm sitting bolt upright, wide awake.

'Mum?'

'Yes.'

'What are you doing here?'

'I'm sitting here for you,' she whispers.

'For me?'

'It's your birthday,' she says mysteriously.

'My birthday?'

'I've got you a present.'

'It's not my birthday at all. And it's still dark.'

From the groan of the basket seat, I can tell she's moving. The bedside lamp flashes on. I screw up my eyes. 'What's going on?'

She's sitting by my bed, where she always used to sit to soothe me when I had a fever and my dreams got scary. Her newly washed hair is twisted up into a knot. 'Get up,' she says.

'But it's not my birthday till June.'

'This year's different. Today you turn fifteen.'

'I'm already fifteen.'

'Who do we have to answer to?'

'No one.'

'Well then. We can celebrate your birthday any time we like.' She yanks the covers off me. 'Come on, get up.'

'It's cold,' I splutter.

'Stop your whining.'

'But it's only quarter to six.'

Reluctantly, I get out of bed. Mum puts her hands to my cheeks and looks up at me. I'm half a head taller. 'Happy birthday.' She presses her lips clumsily to mine and our teeth clunk.

'What are you doing?'

'You're becoming a man. That's something we should celebrate.' She pushes me aside, flops onto my bed, and stretches out. She points her toes, curls up like a foetus, and thumps her head on the pillow a few times. The knot of wet hair leaves dark patches on the pillowcase. 'Fits just fine,' she says, and shoves my pillow off the bed. 'Take that with you.'

'Where to?'

'You can have my room.'

'Your room?'

'You're much too tall for this bed. You'll outgrow your own body soon at this rate.'

'So?'

'This is my present for your birthday.'

It feels weird standing here while she's lying in my bed. 'My birthday isn't till June.'

'Don't be so ungrateful.'

'How d'you mean?'

'Off you go. Be happy with your present.'

'So you're going to sleep up here in the attic from now on?'

She snuggles down and turns her back on me. 'Turn off the lamp, will you? I'm trying to get some sleep here.'

The clock on the oven says 6:13. In a daze, I make myself a bowl of porridge. After two spoonfuls I've had enough and push it aside.

I decide to focus on the stove. A wad of paper, some splinters of wood, and a match. The paper bursts into flames that die out just as quickly. I fish a macaroni box out of the bin. Using a few twigs, I build a little wigwam and hold a match under it. Then another. The cardboard catches light. The twigs turn black, curl up, and collapse. I lay a few strips of wood across the top. Smoke fogs the kitchen, the stove slowly fills with fire, and I push the little door shut.

11

I wake up with one cheek pressed to the table. Mum is flapping a rubbish bag about. The bones in my neck crack.

'We'll never get mine up the stairs,' she says, as if we're in the middle of a conversation.

'What are you talking about?'

'I've tried, but it's much too heavy. We'll have to swap clothes.'

'You mean wardrobes?'

'Mmm.'

Mum has stripped my attic room. The mattress is sagging against the wall and the wardrobe doors are flung wide. The things that stood on my washbasin have been swept into my wastepaper basket. Where my posters once hung there are bare patches of wall, pale as skin that seldom sees the light. Woodworm-sized holes at the corners show where the drawing pins used to be.

'Mikael!' she calls from her old room, one floor below mine.

'Mikael?'

'Mi-ka-el.'

I go down the stairs. Dust swirls through the air in her room. The neat piles from her wardrobe are spread over the floor. With her chin, she pins the neck of a summer dress against her chest.

'You always thought this one was pretty, didn't you?'

I have no idea. She might be right.

'So?'

'What?'

'Does it still look good on me?'

'S'pose.'

'Then I might put it on for you later.'

'It's a bit summery. You'll catch cold.'

'Well, that's up to me, isn't it?'

Under the exposed ribs of her bed I can see a square of crumpled paper tissues, dust, and discarded socks. There's a heap of curtain either side of the window. She sees me looking. 'You can have them, too. They don't fit up in the attic. I should have left them up but I'd already taken them down.'

I nod.

'And this?' She holds up a see-through blouse. 'What do you think of this?' She wrinkles her nose when she asks, so I can't really tell what she wants to hear.

'Uh-hmm,' I mumble.

'Well?' she insists.

I shrug my shoulders.

'What do you think?'

'Maybe not, eh?'

'Uh-huh, that's what I thought.' She stuffs the blouse and the summer dress into a plastic bag that's already overflowing with clothes.

It was a game we played every now and then, when the winter dragged on too long. She'd hold up scarves, I'd pick the prettiest, and she would wrap it around her head. Then she'd let me put lipstick on her lips and she'd lipstick mine. We'd stand in front of the mirror and compare bodies. I had to come up with ten things to prove I was her child. A doctor's frown would appear on her face. 'Out of the question,' she'd say in a mock-serious voice. 'You cannot be my child. That pointy chin is your father's. And you didn't get that willy of yours from me, either. And what about those ears? Look at mine.' She drew back the curtains of hair that concealed them. 'They don't stick out nearly as much as yours and Dad's.'

I would nod patiently, knowing I still had one secret weapon: my belly button. I'd lift my jumper and stick out my tummy. She'd do the same and we'd compare. Both belly buttons were carved with exactly the same apple corer, though it was easier to see the bottom of mine.

'That's ten pieces of evidence in one,' she'd say with a smile. 'So you really are my child?'

'Looks like it,' I said.

'Good, I'm glad.'

I looked so much like Dad you could paste his boyhood pictures into my photo album and not even notice the difference. He sometimes said he had provided the seed and the egg. 'Did not! Did not! Did not!' I'd scream as he pinned me down on the rug and began to tickle me. 'I belong to Mum!' It was only when he grated my face with his prickly chin that I'd surrender.

12

I never want to see that fucking gull again. I'm only going upstairs this once to punish her for the last time. She might think she's stronger than me, but we'll see who's won when I pull the bedroom door shut and lock it so she starves. As I take hold of the handle, I hear high-pitched peeping in among her squawks.

I hesitate.

More peeping.

I let go of the handle, take a handful of stones from my coat pocket, and shuffle into the room. Keeping as close to the door as I can, I stand where I can get a good look at her nest. I scatter the stones across the foot of the bed. A few roll off. Quicker than I expect, the gull waddles across the bed toward them. A chick is sitting at the bottom of her jumbled nest, much too small to peer out over the rim, so small that whenever he turns his head, his whole body turns, too. His feathers are more like stalks, as if he's wearing a chestnut shell. His skin is as translucent and pink as a freshly grazed knee. Hard to imagine his little beak will ever be pointed and white.

The mother gull pecks at the stones, holds them in her beak, then drops them on the bed and goes back and sits on top of her chick. The baby bird worms his way between her and the side of the nest. His little beak pokes up and tries to tap against the red spot on her bill in the hope she'll sick something up into his throat, but he can't reach. As if she can't hear him begging, she turns her head away and roots around among her feathers.

Out by the rocks I go in search of a dead fish or the like. I poke among the seaweed with a branch and stir the flotsam that's gathered on the water lapping between the rocks. Everything I find has been washed clean, picked empty, or stinks so bad I have to hold my breath. I scramble over the boulders and walk halfway round the island till I reach Karl's cooling shed of rusty metal and corrugated iron. The machine that keeps it cold inside hums and rattles. I thrash nettles aside with the branch so I can get closer.

If I ask Karl for a fish, he's bound to call me Master Hammermann and moan on about me not helping him enough.

Under a lean-to at the back of the shed there's a kind of drying rack that he's knocked together out of planks of wood from Miss Augusta's house. Salted haddock, gutted and headless, are drying on the bars like a row of saggy brown stockings. Their scaly skin is tattered and tough, and they're so salty, they can burn a hole in your tongue. I take one of the dried fish and space the others out so it doesn't look like there's one missing. When I fold it in half, the backbone creaks and snaps. I take hold of the hook it was hanging from, twist it out of the tail and throw it in among the clump of birch trees.

It's only been ten minutes, but the gull has already forgotten I was here. I throw the fish onto the bed. 'There you go, shitbag. For that little chick of yours.'

I lock the bedroom door as I leave.

13

I pull my clothes out of the rubbish bag and put them on the empty shelves of Mum's wardrobe. When I'm finished I screw up the bag, go over to Dad's wardrobe, and open the doors. His clothes are neatly stacked in their familiar piles. T-shirts on the left, loose around the neck where he used to hook a finger inside the collar and jiggle it up and down when he was too warm. Next to them are his trousers, and on the right, his jumpers.

I stick my arm between two of the piles and feel along the back of the wardrobe till I find his sunglasses. The lenses flash a sharp reflection and the chewed-up earpieces scratch my temples as I slide them on. Everything in the room takes on a nicotine glaze. In front of the mirror, I tip my head back and brush wisps of hair in front of my ears.

When I put the sunglasses back, I can feel something else lying there. It's Dad's watch. Mum must have put it there. The hands have stopped. I haven't wound it in a long time. I slip it over my wrist and examine it.

Dad had tufts of black hair on his fingers. In the winter the hairs on his right hand were scorched off from putting blocks of wood on the fire. His fingernails were clipped too short and a scar ran down the side of his little finger. I can see it all so precisely, I begin to wonder if I really remember it, or whether I've seen it in a photo.

The shoebox we keep our photos in is up on top of Mum's wardrobe. At the back there's a pile of my baby photos, held together by a rubber band. At the front are the memories from their time together without me, memories I've looked at so often, it's as if I was there. Mum sitting on Dad's lap, fending off the camera with one hand—it's like I could've taken that photograph. Same goes for the photo where he's planting a kiss on her cheek. Or the one of them sitting stiffly side by side, Dad wearing a black suit and sporting a moustache, Mum pressing a bouquet of flowers to her chest, wearing a summer dress and the long earrings that still dangle from her ears sometimes.

Then there's the snapshot where they're leaning across a table in front of a darkened window, raising their glasses to the waiter who's taking the photo. It's the only one where you can see Dad's hands. Wrapped around the stem of his wine glass is the little finger of his left hand.

'What are you up to?'

Startled, I knock the box from my lap. I get down on my knees and start scraping all the photos together, accidentally creasing a few.

'Answer me.' Mum comes and stands beside me, her knees uncomfortably close to my face.

'I was going to ask,' I stammer, 'if you wanted this box upstairs, too.'

'You've got no business rummaging through it.'

'I was only looking.'

'These are not your memories.'

'They're a bit muddled now.'

Mum looks from me to the piles of Dad's clothes.

'Why is the wardrobe open?'

'I was just having a look.'

'His clothes stay exactly where they are.'

'Fine.'

'I don't care what you think.' She thumps up the stairs to the attic and slams the door to my old room. Just as well she didn't see the watch on my wrist.

14

A shoal of cod heads and stringy guts are floating on the shallow waves by the quay. The bodies are hanging on the wooden rack to dry. The smaller ones are tied together by the tail; the heavier ones hang on their own with a shiny hook through the tailfin.

Karl greets me with a nod. 'Come to help?'

'If I can have a fish when I'm finished.'

'We'll see.'

'That big fat mackerel there, maybe. No need to take the head off.'

'Give me a hand first, then we'll see about your just deserts,' he mutters and points to the containers. 'Like with like. And what's not for eating goes back in the sea.'

'You've told me that a hundred times.'

'I must think you're pretty thick, then,' he sniggers, and starts pulling the heads off the cod with his blunt knife. They have a thick curl of fish flesh on their bottom lip, as if their skin has grown over a hook that got stuck in their jaw.

Whenever one of the containers is full, Karl carries it over to the cooling shed, scoops ice over the fish, stacks it on top of the other full containers, and comes back kicking an empty one ahead of him.

I grab a piece of seaweed and sling it as far away as I can.

'There's folk eat that stuff.'

'What?'

'Seaweed.'

'Does it need to go in a container?'

'Chinky food, that is. Gives us the shits.'

I bend over and keep on sorting.

'Runny shite!' Karl hoots.

A little while later he has an eel in his hands. 'Looky here. Usually only get them in my traps.' The eel is still writhing around, and Karl's fist squeezes tight to stop it slipping away.

'Fucking corpse eaters.' He props its mouth open with his thumb. 'Look.' Karl growls like a monster and shoves the eel in my face. 'He'll chomp his way through anything. Lots of folk won't touch 'em cos of that, but me, I'll eat anything. It all turns to shite the next day. It's only the pricey fishies I won't eat. Where's the fun in shitting money?' He takes the writhing eel over to the low wall and smashes its head down on the edge. The eel keeps moving and Karl whacks it against the wall a second time.

'That's more like it.' Slack as rope, the eel slithers into the yellow bucket where Karl keeps the fish he sets aside for himself. 'Supper's sorted.'

He presses his hands into the small of his back and groans as he eases his shoulders back. His fingers are fatter than Dad's, more like sausages.

'Lazy buggers.' Karl nods toward the gulls that have gathered on the quay and the rocks. 'Waiting for one of us to chuck something back into the sea.'

'Dad used to call them sky sailors.'

'Sky sailors? Nothing but bones and stringy meat.'

'You *eat* them?'

'It's a ton of work, and when you're done, you're still hungry.' He brings one hand up to his cheek and stretches the other arm as if aiming a rifle. 'Click, click. Bang. Bang. Bang.' His shouts echo and a couple of gulls take off. He lowers his arm.

'Come on,' he says. 'I'll show you my birds.'

I wipe my hands on my trousers and follow him into the house. In the hallway, wood panels line the ceiling and the walls, which are hung with old photographs and a cross with Jesus on it. It's the kitchen we're heading for. Karl drags over a chair and climbs onto it. On a shelf above the door are a couple of gulls and ducks he's shot and mounted, their backs grey with dust. Karl beams with pride as he takes down one of the gulls. 'Just like the real thing, eh?' There's a strange kink in the neck and wires sticking out of the legs to keep it upright.

'It's got no eyes,' I say.

'D'you have any idea how much them marbles cost?'

'Nope. None.'

'You'll just have to imagine the eyes.' Karl examines his gull proudly from all angles. The head is out of proportion and fishing line is sticking out of the seams where the bird was slit open, scraped hollow, filled, and sewn up again. Karl stuffs them with his own hair. Once Mum has cut it for him, he sweeps it all up with a dustpan and brush. 'No point wasting it when you can use it to stuff a dead duck.' Mum gets an unwelcome kiss on the cheek by way of a thank you.

'Surely a bird like that deserves a place in a natural history museum?' Karl is still towering above me on his chair.

'Hmm.'

'Wouldn't that be a nice little earner. It's not like we're short of 'em round here.'

I walk back outside through the hall, grab the brush, and start sweeping up the last of the seaweed. Karl follows on behind me. 'How much could I get for a stuffed gull, d'you think?'

'How should I know?'

'Two hundred, maybe? Give me a hand and you can earn some extra on the side, too. I must get your mother to cut my hair again soon.'

I lean the brush against the cooling shed. 'Any more jobs you want doing?'

'Now?' Karl takes a look around. 'I reckon we're done.' He nods toward the yellow bucket. 'Take that with you. The eel.'

'I'd rather have a fatter fish.'

'Less than half an hour's work and already he's picking and choosing.'

'Didn't I do a good job?'

'Okay, I'll give you a fat one and the eel's a present from me to your mum.'

I shake my head.

'Getting all picky again?'

'Mum can't stand eels.'

15

Down here the ceiling is square and flat instead of sloped, but the house sounds almost the same as it did from my attic room. I fall back on the bed to the noise of groaning springs. You used to be able to see a kind of shark in the little cracks on the ceiling. Dad would get me to lie down next to him and I'd watch as he traced the outline with his finger. 'Upside-down fishing' I called it.

It was like when he showed me constellations up in the sky.

'Yes! Now I can see it,' I'd say, even if I couldn't. 'What's that one called?'

'The Great Bear.'

'But you just told me it looks like a saucepan.'

'We made all this up ourselves.'

'Who did?'

'Mankind.'

'Are we part of mankind?'

'Not me,' he said. 'You?'

'Nah, 'course not.' If Dad wasn't part of it, then neither was I. 'Does Mum belong to mankind?'

'*She* does, yes.'

'Cos she can do town talk?'

His belly wobbled but his laugh was silent. 'Don't go telling her that or she'll think I put the idea in your head.'

'You did.'

'Yeah, but she doesn't need to know that.'

Cos it was my bedtime I thought up another question. 'So what else did mankind make up?'

'How d'you mean?'

'You said mankind made up that stuff about the stars.'

'Oh, right. Those stars don't really belong together at all. Stars don't even know other stars exist. And they certainly don't know they're part of a group with a name.' When we stood outside at night and looked up, we whispered in case the stars got a fright and flew away.

'Can I sleep next to you tonight?'

'Mum's got that spot booked already.'

Above me I can hear footsteps and the sound of something big being dragged across the floor. It could be my wardrobe or else my bed. I want to know what she's up to in my old room but I don't have the nerve to knock when she's in there, and when she's not, the door is locked. I roll onto her side of the bed and then back onto Dad's side. After a while, I get up.

Out on the landing, my things are huddled by the door, looking awkward and out of place. My collection of shells. A jar of feathers I saved. The contents of my desk drawer in a pillowcase: drawing pins, paper clips, pens, a rubber, letters, stickers, and my Swiss Army knife. Rolled-up posters. The red football, getting soft around the edges. A tower of schoolbooks, my atlas, and comics I've read so often they're falling apart. The wastepaper basket with my brush, toothpaste, and deodorant lying on a bed of scrunched-up paper and used cotton buds. There's the beanbag Dad made for me. My binoculars. I've no idea how she managed to get my desk down the attic stairs, but it's here, too. Up in my old room they were my world, my only possessions. Now they're out here looking so lost, it makes me feel a weird kind of homesick.

16

Tomato sauce colours her whole head red, as if she's just buried her beak deep inside a dead seal. Her back and her wings are spattered red, too. She gulps down all the macaroni in the plastic dish. The chick has climbed over the edge of the nest and is peeping and scrabbling around over the bed behind her. His skin is covered with a fuzzy stubble as speckled as the egg he hatched from. He gets too close to his mother and she accidentally knocks him over with her tail.

When she turns to smother his peeping, the little bird tries to tap the red spot on her beak, though it's still way too high for him. The mother gull raises her wings a little and stretches her neck. There's a spasm or two, and she sicks up a couple of times into the chick's wide-open throat. She does the same twice over.

I want to feed him, too. On my guard, I drag the plastic dish toward me with a coat hanger. The mother leers at me, the corners of her bill turned down in that grouchy expression all gulls share. Her head is alert and follows my every move. I scrape together what's left of the macaroni and pick it up with my fingers.

As calmly as I can, I edge round the bed to get closer to her chick. He scrambles around hungrily but doesn't understand that I'm trying to feed him. Even when I'm only a few feet away, he keeps ignoring me and begging food from his mother. She's positioned herself between us so she can keep an eye on me without losing sight of her chick. I try to lure him over by clicking my tongue, and hold my macaroni-covered fingers out to him. I click again. The little gull seems to notice me and turns around. In a flash, the mother rears up and snatches the macaroni. Nerves jangling, I spit out an angry 'sssss'. The peck from her beak tingles in my fingertips. 'That wasn't meant for you.'

The chick stands in front of his mother and opens his beak wide but she ignores him. When she settles back on her nest, he burrows underneath her.

I slam the bedroom door behind me.

17

Waking in the middle of the night, I can't understand why the floor to the left of my bed is striped with moonlight. At first I think I'm lying the wrong way round, and I start to turn. Then I can't understand why the ceiling above me is square and flat instead of sloped. Then I remember where I am.

The flushing of the toilet in the bathroom has woken me, followed by the sound of water gushing through the pipes in the wall. I listen to the landing groan under Mum's feet. From here it sounds almost the same as in my old room. I expect to hear the attic stairs creak next, but they don't make a sound. Instead I hear my door open.

'Mum?' My hand gropes around for the light cord above my bed. She hits the switch by the door at exactly the same moment and the ceiling light flashes on and off in a heartbeat. I catch a snapshot of her in a washed-out nightshirt, her back to me, legs lit up, finger by the light switch. Then it goes dark again.

'Huh...' she mumbles drowsily. 'Broken.' I slowly let go of the cord and the fluorescent bead on the end swings to and fro against the wallpaper. 'Broken,' she mumbles again. In the dark, I hear her feet shuffling toward her side of the bed. Air rushes under the covers as she lifts them up and rolls onto the mattress. I make myself as small as I can.

'Warm,' she sighs. 'Nice warm bed.' She tugs at the covers and I feel the sheet drag across my stomach. I'm lying at the edge of the bed, as far from her as I can get. Muscles tensed, I try to halt the rise and fall of my chest, arms stiff at my sides. I listen to all the little sounds of her breathing. I swear I can hear the flicker of her eyelashes. Each time I take a breath, it whistles in my ears like the wind through the window. When I swallow, it's enough to shake the bed. Mum turns onto her side. I want to get up and go up to my old room, but the warmth of the bed keeps me under the covers. Mum's breathing slows and deepens.

She's lying so close she's almost pushing me onto the floor, but her nearness makes the thought of the cold mattress up in the attic even colder.

This isn't my fault. It's hers. I was sleeping and she came and lay down next to me. I didn't even notice. She can't pin the blame on me in the morning.

Her teeth grind gently.

How could I know what was happening? I was sound asleep. It's her mistake. I'll insist I was asleep. My clasped hands relax and I sink a little deeper into the mattress.

There's a rock-a-bye motion in the slow sighs of Mum's breathing, like the soothing rush of water flowing into a bath, the gurgle of the coffee maker, the lazy chug of our washing machine.

I wake up to find an empty space beside me. I'm lying in the middle of the bed. On Mum's side a long stretch of blanket has slid onto the floor. It's morning.

I run my hand over the mattress but feel no difference in temperature. The bedroom door is half open. The ceiling light snaps on as soon as I pull the cord. No surprise there.

I can feel a restless ache in my belly. As I slept, she woke up in this bed. Shocked at waking up beside me, or maybe even angry, she got up without a word. If I say anything, she'll know I knew. Her mistake will be my fault, after all. I should have gone and slept somewhere else, or at least have woken her up. I can't let on I've noticed anything.

Down in the kitchen she's standing at the sink, dunking a teabag in a steaming pot of tea. I walk over and stand beside her, yawn conspicuously, and start stacking plates and pans as if I'm going to do the washing up. A fly lands on the draining board and starts cleaning itself. Mum sees it, too. She holds the dripping teabag still above the pot. 'Go for it,' she whispers to me.

I hook my forefinger behind the tip of my thumb and steer my hand steadily across the kitchen counter toward the fly. My other three fingers are raised. It's a trick Dad taught me. Whenever the fly's legs stop moving and it freezes, you have to keep your hand still. When it goes on cleaning itself, you can glide your finger and thumb closer in one smooth motion.

The fly freezes twice, and I stop my hand just in time. Thumb and finger are primed for action, now just a fraction from the fly. I glance at Mum. She's lost in concentration, staring cat-like at my fingers and the fly. Wham! I flick it past the teapot and off the counter. It hits the floor with a tick and disappears among the grimy dust under the oven.

Mum gives me a triumphant look. 'Bullseye!' she says. 'In one go, too.' She raises the teapot high in the air. 'This calls for a cuppa!'

I take my mug from among the dirty dishes and she fills it to just under the brim. 'Thanks,' I say, and go to pick it up.

'Hang on! My lion tamer deserves a little extra.' She tops it up with three more splashes from the teapot. 'And... one last little drop,' she says and the mug overflows. A brown puddle forms on the counter. 'There you go.'

I can't pick up the mug without tea spilling over the sides.

'What do you say?'

'Thank you,' I reply, and bend forward to blow on the tea.

'That was clever of you.' She goes over and sits at the table. There's something supple in her words and movements, like they're dancing. It's going to be a good day.

'Can you reach the radio?'

'D'you want me to turn it on?'

'Please. Let's get nice and cosy in here.'

With one knee on the counter and my arm stretched as far as it will go, I can just reach the radio on top of the cupboard. It's caked in grime and dust, and the lead is wrapped around it. I plug it in and the little red light comes on. After I've turned the dial for a while, a song breaks through the crackle and hiss. 'Shall I leave it on this channel?'

'You choose.'

Now I start to wonder whether she really likes it or not. I twiddle the dial again, but this is the only channel that comes through loud and clear. 'I'll leave it on this one, okay?'

We blow on our tea. A fly's wing is stuck to my fingernail. It's so light I can't even feel it.

18

Karl picks up a long knife with a jagged edge and saws a washed-up lump of polystyrene foam into big blocks. Dust snows all around us. It's my job to hold the polystyrene while Karl slices through it. When that's done, he grabs an awl and punches holes in the blocks. 'Stick that lot through the middle till just over halfway.' 'That lot' are the thick reeds he's collected. The leaves that still cling to the stalks carve shallow cuts in my fingers. In a little while he'll attach these floats to his traps, so they're easier to find around the island. Anyone going swimming should really fasten one of these contraptions to their waist.

'Right then, time for a smoke.' While he fumbles for his cigarettes, I pull out my pack, casual as can be.

'Here,' I say. 'I think there's a couple left.' I've been waiting for this moment ever since I nabbed them from Miss Augusta's kitchen drawer.

'Well, get this!' says Karl, surprised. 'Handing out smokes now, are we?'

'Isn't it about time?'

'True, that scrounging of yours was getting beyond a joke.'

I nudge a cigarette out of the pack with my thumb and offer it to him, exactly like I've rehearsed it up in my room.

'Lavanda filter tips for the ladies. Now there's a blast from the past.'

'Does it make a difference?'

'A ciggie's a ciggie.'

I take the other one and slide the empty pack into my trouser pocket. I like the way the sharp corners feel against my leg. When I walk along, it lets me know it's there with every step.

'Are they your mother's?' he says, puffing out smoke and inhaling another lungful.

'Mum doesn't smoke.'

'An old pack of your dad's?'

I shake my head.

'Lavanda haven't looked like that in a long time.' He takes the cigarette from between his lips. 'Show me that pack again.'

I fish it out of my pocket.

'Are these from Pernille's?'

I nod.

'Lain there all this time?'

I give another nod and he hands me the pack.

'Ripe for a museum, that is.'

'Was she your girlfriend?'

'Pernille?' Karl splutters. 'Let's just say she was a friend.'

'A lady friend?'

'Just a friend. You heard me. Old and dead.'

'She was a kind of grandma.'

'Not back then, she wasn't.'

'How old were you when you went with her?'

'How d'you know all this, anyway?'

'Miss Augusta told me once.'

'Told *you*?'

'And Dad.'

We're leaning on the low wall and looking out to sea. Karl scratches under his woolly hat. 'A woman's a woman, sonny. Hands, feet, and holes in all the right places. That's all it takes.'

'So?'

'Listen.' He sticks his calloused hands out in front of him as if to show how big a loaf is. 'You've got a man.' He wiggles his left hand. 'And you've got a woman.' He waggles his right. 'On one island.' He slams his hands together. 'If you're cooped up together long enough, any woman will do. Same the other way round, though that usually takes a bit longer.'

I take a step back so I'm out of his reach and wipe my nose on my sleeve.

'So the two of you had sex together?'

'Nah, we sipped tea and discussed the price of herring.'

'You can tell me, can't you?'

'You're a little shit, you know that,' says Karl with a flash of his dull yellow teeth. 'And just like your dad. He was always banging on about stuff like this, too.'

I've smoked my cigarette down to the filter and flick it

in the direction of the bramble bushes. Little balls of polystyrene are suspended in Karl's hair.

'Sounds like you need a trip to Ladyville.'

'Maybe.'

'You know what they say: hair on your lip, time for a dip.' His laugh rasps around the edges. My face turns bright red and I pull my collar up under my nose.

'In Ladyville you can grab a girl and try it all out for yourself. No need to ask the guy next door how it all works.'

I want to distract him with another cigarette, but my pack is empty. 'I've already had a shag. Ages ago.'

'You?' Karl glares at me in disbelief. 'Who with? Yer mother?'

''Course not.'

'Don't try and tell me you've had yer end away. I'm not buying it for a second.'

I kick away an old washer. It leaves behind a rusty ring on the concrete.

'And don't go shaving that bumfluff off before I take you to town or they'll never believe you're over eighteen.' He thumps me on the shoulder. 'Tip from your old neighbour.'

Off in the distance, shafts of sunlight pierce the clouds and shed a faint light across the sea. Karl starts to gather up his tools and gauges the weight of a jerrycan to see how much petrol's left in it.

'Does your mum know?'

'Know what?'

'About Pernille and me.'

'You mean about her being your girlfriend?' I say, just to piss him off.

'Remind me to keep my ciggies to myself in future.' He pokes me in the ribs. 'You know fine and well what

I'm getting at, Hammermann.'

'I don't think so.'

'Good,' says Karl. 'The ladies can get pretty jealous about that kind of thing. Even when the competition's snuffed it ages ago.'

'My mum's not one of your ladies. And she couldn't care less about you and Miss Augusta.'

'Ah! That's cos she doesn't know,' Karl grins. 'So let's keep it that way.' He sniffs noisily and spits over the wall. 'Every mother's a woman deep down. And yours is no exception, that's for sure.'

19

Mum does know. Dad told her all about it.

It was late one autumn. I remember how marshy the ground was and the way the mosquitoes were swarming above the little pools that had formed everywhere. The sun was low in the sky and turned the kitchen orange. I was sitting under Miss Augusta's table and came out cos she'd put extra biscuits on the plate. Dad had just finished gluing a chair leg or re-hanging a painting, and was absent-mindedly tracing a fingernail along the grain of the tabletop. Without either of them seeing, I snatched two biscuits. After a long silence, Miss Augusta said, 'Karl and I have a history.'

'A history?' Dad asked without looking up.

'Long before you came to live here with Dora.'

'Are the two of you related?'

'No. There were always two families. Both fisherfolk. Each with their own half of the island.'

'Karl's mentioned that before.'

'Our history began after all that.'

'After?'

'He was a child and I was a good bit older. We didn't have much in common. Until he became a man and suddenly discovered I was a woman.'

Dad frowned. 'And then?'

'I'm sure you get the picture, Birk.'

'And that's when your history began?'

'Karl and I found each other.'

'Karl and... you?'

Miss Augusta nodded and stirred her coffee.

'Pernille?'

'Yes.'

'You're making this up, aren't you?'

'Don't you believe me?'

'Karl doesn't strike me as your type. And there's quite an age difference between you.'

'Nothing love couldn't overcome.'

'Was it love?'

Miss Augusta got up to put a block of wood in the round iron stove, though there was no need; she'd done the same thing only minutes before. A cloud of smoke billowed through the kitchen. 'Karl thought I was teaching him everything, but it was as new to me as it was to him.' Miss Augusta sat back down on her chair and picked bits of fluff from her skirt. 'We were young. At least, Karl was young, and his father died. I was still without a husband. And then, all of a sudden.' The corners of her mouth tried to suppress a smile. 'Now he wants nothing more to do with me, but back then it was a different story.'

'Jeez,' said Dad.

'For me, a table had only ever been for eating at, but I soon discovered it had more uses than that.'

Dad's roar of laughter bounced around the kitchen. He laid his arm on the back of my chair.

'More coffee?'

'Next time, Pernille. We'd better be getting back to Mum.'

'Yes, you two need to get back to Mum,' said Miss Augusta, and gave me a couple of pats on the back.

'Now don't be in too much of a hurry to break something else,' said Dad.

Miss Augusta chuckled. 'I'll do my best.'

As we walked back home through the rising mist, Dad said, 'You mustn't tell anyone else what Miss Augusta told us.'

'What exactly did she say, again?'

He took my hand and gave it a squeeze. 'Shall we go and find a crab for Mum? Then she can make us some soup.'

That night in bed, he told her himself. Mum squealed a couple of times in disgust and Dad had to ssssst her to be quiet. 'No way! You're kidding,' she repeated, laughing like she was being tickled. 'It can't be true, it can't.'

Then their light went out, and after a while the bed began to squeak. Dad had told me their bed squeaked when they couldn't get to sleep and they were both tossing and turning under the covers. I couldn't sleep either, but my bed didn't make any noise unless I jumped up and down on it, and it was usually too cold on top of the blanket for that.

20

The gold letters on the leather cover are faded and the pages are dotted with fungus around the edges. The encyclopaedia has nothing to say about your first shag. And under 'moustache' it only lists the different kinds, and I can't find mine on the list. There's nothing about bumfluff, either.

Now that I've got the E-to-M volume down off the shelf, I sit down in Dad's chair with my legs dangling over the arm. I flick past 'maggots', 'maidenhead', 'microscope', and 'moon'. Back toward the beginning, I find something about gulls. There aren't any photos but there are some drawings of beaks. There's also a bit about which birds belong to the gull family. They eat carrion but also hunt live prey, including all kinds of fish, and sometimes crabs. All it says about the chicks is that they're fully formed when they hatch and that they can't digest their own food for the first couple of weeks, so their mother has to eat it first. I picture Mum eating her bowl of chewed-up rope and then throwing it all up so she can feed it to me. I'm glad I'm not a gull.

The last volume of the encyclopaedia contains the V words, and there's a little drawing of a vagina. I always have to take a look, even though it makes me feel a bit queasy. It's like looking inside a body through a wound that hasn't been sewn up right. A little arrow points out the entrance to the vagina in among the sinews and lobes of flesh. It's a kind of dark mouse hole that makes you so curious you want to stick your finger in, but you don't dare cos you're afraid something might bite you.

I browse further to the bit about Venus statues. When I look at those pictures it's easier to remember what Miss

Augusta looked like. The same stocky body with reined-in rolls of fat, but then in a flowery dress, with gold-coloured spectacles perched on her nose, and veins running riot up her legs.

The back of this thick book is where we keep my swimming certificate, so it won't get creased. Dad drew it for me when he decided I had passed the swimming lessons he gave me. *Official testimony that Mikael Hammermann can swim* is written in curly letters with a massive swirly signature at the bottom. *B. Hammermann* is printed underneath.

21

'Clear off, stupid bird.'

Gull stays put on the seat of the chair. I swing the door wider and scatter another handful of mussels on the landing, closer to the staircase this time. A few of the shells tumble over the edge and tick against the stairs on their way down. Gull squawks at me but her gaze is fixed on the landing. She turns this way and that, drops from the chair, and steps hesitantly over the threshold. As soon as she does I kick the door shut. 'Don't be afraid,' I say to the peeping sound coming from under the bed. 'It's only me.' The gull chick has taken refuge between the legs of the bed and the wall.

An image of me stepping on the panicky chick as he shoots out into the open flashes into my mind and makes me extra-careful. In slow motion I bring my heel down on a couple of mussels and stand on them with my full weight. They crack. One by one I pick the fleshy orange pouches from their shells and pull off the stringy bits of beard. I wipe them clean on my trouser leg and put them in my mouth. Uncooked, the mussels are a rubbery mouthful of sea, with grit that grinds against my teeth. The sudden thought that I'm chewing on the vagina from the encyclopaedia brings a sour taste to my mouth. I breathe through my nose a couple of times and munch on determinedly, then push the paste onto my palm with my tongue. Even when a mussel's whole it's hard to tell what you're looking at, but this mush really could be anything. I spit on the ground a few times. The grit continues to set my teeth on edge.

Out on the landing the mother gull is screeching and tapping her beak against the door. Under the bed I can hear the restless peeping and scrambling of her chick. I get down on my knees. 'Look what I've got for you,' I say to soothe him. To start with, I take a little of the chewed mussels between thumb and finger and reach out my arm. 'Come on.' I calmly edge the mussel mush in his direction. 'Don't be afraid.' It takes a while before he summons the courage to come closer. His fuzzy plumage has become a little thicker and he has more control over his head. He's grown quicker than I expected. By withdrawing my hand little by little, I lure him out from under the bed. 'There you go. See. No need to be afraid.'

He taps his beak against the red button on the cuff of my coat. I hold the chewed mussels above him. He flaps the stumps that will soon be his wings and even takes a little jump in an attempt to reach my fingers. With every cry, the tip of his pointy little tongue sticks out.

Carefully I push a little of the mush into his warm gullet on the tip of my little finger. Immediately he gives another peep. I take some more mush and push my finger in a little deeper. If I don't pull back straight away, I can feel him swallow. Even the thought that I could kill him at any moment makes me feel guilty.

I divide the last little helping of mussels into two portions and feed them to him. I show him my empty hands, but of course he doesn't understand.

'You will be mine.' I whisper the words, though there's no one around who might hear. 'You will be all mine.' He runs his beak awkwardly across the fuzz on his back and pecks at the wooden floor, exactly like his mother does. More than anything, I want to stroke his head for a while and feel the softness of his speckled downy feathers. But I resist the urge to touch him. 'Then your mother won't want you anymore. She'll think you smell too much of me.'

When I open the door the mother gull attacks the toes of my boots. I could kick her if I wanted to, but she darts past my legs and into the room.

Once I've pulled the door shut I make sure it will stay closed. 'See you tomorrow,' I whisper to my chick. 'And if not, the day after.'

22

There are traps to be emptied, so here we are, bobbing around the island in a little wooden boat. It's so leaky I have to bail almost non-stop, scooping out the water in a milk carton with the top cut off.

'This one's just about had it,' said Karl as he hung the little motor over the back. 'But we don't need to go far from shore.'

Wherever he sees a reed or a twig sticking out of a polystyrene block in the water, he brings the boat to a halt while the motor chunters away. Karl's lumbering movements send us rocking dangerously from side to side. He squeezes past me and sinks to his knees with a groan. Right sleeve rolled up, his arm disappears into the water and pulls on a rope to hoist up the trap. He opens it and caged eels spill out onto the bottom of the boat, squirming like live spaghetti. I tuck my feet up out of the way; Karl tramples them underfoot without a second thought.

He's set two traps in the water over by Miss Augusta's house. I look up at the window of the bedroom where my chick is waiting. Karl looks at the house, too, and shakes his head. 'There's no stopping 'em. Those fucking birds shit on everything.'

He clamps the rudder between his knees to stop the waves from driving our leaky boat onto the rocks. From his breast pocket he produces a fresh pouch of tobacco. Once he's rolled his own, I automatically hold out my hand. He takes a miserly look at the full pouch and sighs. 'On you go, then. Just the one.' He tosses it over. 'Next time bring yer own smokes, Master H.'

In silence I roll the cigarette paper and light it. The result looks more like an ice-cream cone than a cigarette.

'We had some good times in there.' Karl sniggers. 'If those walls could talk.'

'What would they say?'

'All sorts.' He licks his lips till they're wet. 'Things you already know way too much about.'

Suddenly the motor splutters to a halt. Karl stands up and yanks the cord till it throbs into life again. He turns the throttle furiously and a thick grey cloud settles around us. Shallow waves slap against the bow.

'D'you know what I tried once?' asks Karl.

'Nope.'

'A few years ago I hung dead gulls by their legs around the house to scare the others off. But they're not afraid of anything.'

I remember seeing the dead gulls dangling from the gutter and the trees. I thought Karl had hung them there to keep me away. Swaying around in the wind, it was almost like they were flying. Their feathers were dirty and their staring eyes were dull as dead jellyfish. I only dared go past again when they'd been eaten away and there were only strings left hanging from the branches.

Karl sighs. 'Shame no one wants to live here.'

'How d'you mean?'

'I asked around town a few times. But...' He sniffs and shakes his head. 'Maybe I should offer free board for fixing it up. At least then the place would be lived in again.'

A shock runs through my body. 'That's not allowed.'

'Not allowed?'

'I don't want anyone coming to live here.'

'Oh. And that's your decision, is it?'

'It's my house.'

'Your house?'

'I go over there and so did Dad.'

'First of all, it was Pernille's house, and when she snuffed it the whole shebang became mine.'

'But you said she wasn't your wife.'

'Who said?'

'You said.'

'Everything over there is rotting away to nothing. If I can make a bit of money out of it, I will. And if there's a tasty young lass who wants the place for free, that's more than fine with me. Then there'll be two ladies on this island for me to feast my eyes on.'

'That house is mine.' My voice is shaking. 'No one's allowed in there.'

'Exactly what do you get up to in that dump?'

'None of your business.'

'Right. You listen here. It's all one to me if you go over there now and then, but the place belongs to me. And if I find someone who wants to live there, you've got one choice: accept it.'

I feel like I'm going to cry but I blink till the mist vanishes.

'Get the message?'

I want to grab something and whack Karl on his fat head, shove him overboard, and make sure his hand gets caught in the propeller blades. 'That house is mine,' I say under my breath.

'Can't make out what you're saying, matey, but I trust I've made myself clear.'

The little motor sputters us over to the rest of the traps. I've forgotten to keep bailing; a pool has formed at the bottom of the boat and the eels are writhing about. I drag the milk carton through the water a few times but their slithering makes me feel sick and angry. I catch flashes of evil pinhead eyes and those pointed teeth that gnaw through dead bodies. I trap one beneath my heel and crush its head. All that's left is a bloody pulp that bears the imprint of my boot.

23

Clean clothes are festooned along the washing line between the shed and our house, fluttering in the breeze.

There's something hopeful about them, as if the garden has been decked out for a party. Mum is wearing her apron and taking in the washing. The basket on the grass at her feet is already half full. Only they're not our clothes, they're Dad's.

'Why are his clothes hanging all over the place?'

Mum smiles when she notices me. With one hand she lets two clothes pegs slide into her apron pocket, in the other she holds out a shirt. I take it from her and press the pearly plastic buttons through the little eyes in the fabric. I pull the collar tight between my fingertips, but the wrinkles keep returning. With my back to the wind I try to fold it as neatly as possible.

'Thank you,' she says as I hand her the shirt. Instead of adding it to the pile in the washing basket, she flaps it open. She pegs the shirt to my shoulders with her fingers and holds it against my chest. It smells of our new washing powder. 'Here's one you don't wear often,' she says, and nods to me to put my fingers where hers are. Screwing up her eyes, she gathers in a few inches of fabric at the waist, exactly like when she's sitting at her sewing machine. Except now it's words not pins between her lips. 'Well, answer me.'

'Answer what?'

'Why don't you wear it more often? It's still in good condition.'

I feel the fluff on the collar against my lower lip. She peers through her lashes, takes the fabric between her fingers, and presses it against my sides. Then she tugs sharply till I let it go and takes it indoors. 'It's Dad's!' I shout after her.

Distant clouds rumble. Steel cables ping against the mast of Karl's cutter and trees shake leaves from their branches. I feel a first raindrop on my neck, then one on my arm, another on my cheek. I pull Dad's socks from the clothesline and have to run to get the washing basket inside while it's still dry.

I put everything back in Dad's wardrobe, in roughly the same piles as before. Up in the attic I can hear the rattling of her sewing machine.

That evening I find two frayed strips of cloth in the rubbish bin. It's only when I go to bed that I notice she's hooked a coat hanger on the handle of my bedroom window. There's the shirt, dark-blue stitching running down both sides. All my altered clothes are scarred with the same thread.

I lay the shirt on my bed, arms spread wide. The alteration makes the fabric pucker around the buttons. I cross the sleeves over the chest and Dad's shirt seems to hug itself. Then I fold it in half and hide it in the middle of a pile. That way it looks like nothing's changed.

24

The ground tries to squelch my boots to a standstill at every step. The rain is so heavy I can barely see more than ten feet ahead. The rectangles of Karl's windows are the only light amid the grey. I try to carry all three of our crates down to the quay in one go, struggling to keep my balance on the slippery grass. In the places where the grass has been washed away, streams of water twist down the slope toward the sea.

'Get a move on, will you? I'm getting soaked here.'

Ingmar is waiting impatiently for me at the bow. As soon as I see him I forget the rain. 'You're back!'

'What did you expect?'

'You know, just your dad on his own.' I throw the empty crates over the rail, hand him our shopping list, and take our groceries from him.

'You won't be seeing much more of my dad.'

'How come?'

'This is his last run.'

'Is he sick?'

Ingmar shakes his head. 'He'll be out and about with his tourists. I'm doing this round from now on.'

'Really?'

'Got ourselves another boat. He'll be taking that one out.'

'Will he bring them here, too?'

'Here?' Ingmar snorts. 'This isn't what folk want to see. Here you might as well be dead. Another mile or two and you drop off the planet.'

'Less chat, ladies!' Brigitta bellows from the cabin.

Ingmar wipes the rain from his face with the back of his hand. 'Cheerio then.'

'You're getting a moustache,' I say.

He looks at me, wide-eyed. 'That's rich, coming from you.'

When Ingmar tries to go into the cabin, his dad blocks the doorway and leaves him standing in the rain. 'Wanna get past?' Brigitta grins broadly, raising his fists like a boxer and hopping from side to side. Ingmar copies him and thumps him a couple of times in the belly. 'Hah! Is that yer best shot?' taunts Brigitta. Now Ingmar leans in with his full weight and gets laid into him. His dad barely flinches and grabs Ingmar by the arm. 'Those biceps o' yours are fair comin' along,' he chuckles, 'but yer old dad's still the strong man around here.' With a feint,

Ingmar slips past him into the cabin. The portholes are all misted up. I raise a hand to Brigitta.

'See you around.'

'Cheerio, lad. Give my regards to that mother of yours.'

25

I rummage around among the bits and pieces on the workbench till I find a screwdriver. I jam the end under the lip of the lid and lever it up and down a few times to prise the tin open. The layer of paint at the bottom is tough as elastic.

There's also a bucket of pitch, some varnish, the white paint that's on the beams in the living room, the black that's on the floors, and a tin of red enamel Mum used to paint over a curved chest of drawers that once belonged to Miss Augusta. All the paint has dried up except the enamel. It's thick as honey but the tin is still half full.

Hidden among the paint tins, I discover Dad's old toolbox. It contains nuts and bolts, sorted according to type. I put a couple of stray nuts back in the right compartment. There's also a hammer with a new handle Dad carved himself from a piece of wood, and a pair of pincers. I slip the pincers into my back pocket so I can use them to pull some nails out of my bedroom wall. I also find a tin of shoe polish, some wire, connector strips, and a roll of sticking plaster with a couple of dark spots of blood on the end. His blood.

In this toolbox, it's as if he's still alive. Everything was lying there exactly as he'd left it. Hurriedly I begin to put everything back. It all has to go back, exactly as it was before I opened it. The stray nuts in the wrong compartments. The roll of plaster with the dark blood spots on top of that. The hammer. I can't remember exactly where everything went. My hands tremble as I press the lid shut and shove the toolbox back among the paint tins.

I start to run. I skirt the house, squeeze through the bushes, and head out into the field in the middle of the island. I stand there panting. The pincers are jabbing into my backside. I take them out of my pocket and pinch one of my fingertips till it turns white, then purple, and then goes numb. The cold wind makes my ears burn. I fling the pincers away.

Karl's cutter appears in the distance. Gulls circle around the highest point as if they're expecting fish to rain down from the sky. Karl must have seen me, cos he gives two short blasts on his horn. I turn and run down toward the back of the island. As food for my gull chick, I pull some mussels from the rocks along the way.

I wait till it's dark before I go back home.

26

I wipe the mist from the bathroom mirror with my towel. When I tilt my head backward, the point of my Adam's apple sticks out a little. The mirror mists over again.

Suddenly the door handle jerks and the latch rattles. 'Why is this door locked?'

'Hang on a sec.'

'What are you doing?'

'I'm finished.' As soon as I lift the latch the door flies open. Fingers clamped around the door handle, Mum gives me a searching look. She's wearing knickers and one of the baggy T-shirts she sleeps in.

'What were you doing?'

'I've just had a bath.'

'You took your time about it.'

'How d'you mean?' I can feel warmth flush my cheeks.

'You should open the top window when you get out of the bath.' Mum squeezes past me, drops her knickers past her knees, and sits on the toilet. As her pee gushes, she looks up at me and smiles. Ever since I was a child, the stream of her piss has been one of the most unsettling noises I know.

'D'you want me to do it?'

'What?'

'Shave off that moustache of yours.'

I feel my upper lip. 'It's about time,' she says. She tears a length of toilet paper from the roll, crumples it into a wad and wipes between her legs. I look away a second too late.

From behind the mirrored door of the bathroom cabinet she takes Dad's old razor and brandishes it between her fingers. 'But Karl says I'll look much younger without it.'

'And I say you're prickling me with it.'

I shrug my shoulders.

'May I?'

I nod half-heartedly.

'Good,' she says and turns the tap on so full, it splashes over the side of the basin. Using her wrist to test the water temperature, she takes a dried-out piece of shaving soap from the cabinet and holds it under the tap till it begins to foam.

'Bend your knees, otherwise I can't reach properly.' Now that her face is close to mine, I can smell everything she says. One hand grips my neck tightly, the other finger-paints my upper lip with foam. Her breath squeaks through her nose and tickles my throat and chest. I suppress a shiver. The razor makes short passes over my upper lip, tugging at the hairs. 'These blades are too old,' she mutters, but keeps on shaving.

Instead of telling me what to do, she sticks her nose in the air, twists her mouth to one side, and clamps her lips together. I copy her expressions. Then she smears some foam on my cheeks. 'Next time, when you do this by yourself, always pull the razor in the same direction as the hairs first and then go against the grain once.'

'Okay,' I mumble.

'Otherwise you'll get little bumps.'

I nod.

'Head still.'

'Sorry.'

Her hand squeezes my neck even tighter.

'A fine job, if I say so myself,' she says finally. 'What do you think?'

'Fine,' I say. A little nick just below my lip is bleeding. She sees I've noticed.

'These razor blades are old,' she says.

'That's all right.'

'It was the blades.'

'Okay.'

'Press this against it.'

I lick away the blood and crumple up the sheet of toilet paper she hands me.

'Do you really like it?'

I begin to nod, as if she's done something wonderful. 'Really good, honest.'

Mum grins broadly. 'Told you I'm good at shaving.' Quick as a flash she hooks two fingers under the waistband of my underpants, tugs, and lets the elastic snap back against my hip. Without another word she leaves the bathroom, pulling the door closed behind her.

I look at myself up close in the mirror and let the soapy water drain away. It leaves a foamy rim specked with almost-invisible stubble.

My tongue is best for feeling the strange new skin around my lips. Stiff and smooth at the same time. It smells a bit like Dad.

Out on the landing, Mum is blocking the way to my room and holding something behind her back. A bright idea is gleaming in her eyes. 'Now put this on.' She holds up one of Dad's jumpers.

The sight of it gives me a start.

'The colour matches your hair.'

'I've already got a jumper.' It's all I can think of to say. 'It's still clean. I only put it on yesterday.'

She presses the jumper against my chest as if she's trying to slap a sticker on me. 'Don't tell me I took it in for nothing.'

'It's way too big for me.'

'Put. It. On.' She starts to force the neck of the jumper down over my head. As she pulls it down roughly, her nail scratches the skin next to my eye.

'Ow! Give over!' I yell, louder than I need to. 'I don't want it.'

'Ungrateful little sod.'

'It's not mine.'

She pins me to the wall with her knee. 'You are going to put this on. Now.'

I try to push her away, but I can't. 'You shouldn't touch Dad's things. They should stay his.'

She freezes and her hands let go of me. I pull the jumper off my head. Mum's eyes are wide. Her cheeks are two dents in her face. She disappears into the bathroom and slams the door so hard the frame groans. I stand there on the landing, the jumper hanging limp in my hands. It had been a birthday present for Dad. Mum had worked on it in secret, knitting a little every evening when she came up to tuck me in. When she was done for the night, I had to return it to its hiding place under my bed. Once Dad's was finished, I wanted her to make the same jumper for me, but with a plane on the front instead of an anchor. I pointed out a pattern in one of the knitting magazines I'd found at Miss Augusta's. She started on the sleeves, but that was about as far as she got. She ran out of wool and kept forgetting to order more. Eventually she unpicked the sleeves and rolled the yarn back into a ball.

The jumper itches and pricks like nettles brushing against my back and stomach. It's too wide and the sleeves hang down over my hands. 'I've put it on,' I say softly. 'Come and see.'

It's quiet in the bathroom.

'I'm sorry. I've put it on now.' I press my ear to the door, on my guard in case she suddenly yanks it open. 'Mum?' I whisper, so close to the door I almost kiss the wood.

It's as if she's no longer there, as if she's climbed out the top window. 'Mum?' She'd never fit through a window that size. She must still be in there.

'Mum?' Perhaps she's on the toilet or shaving her legs or... 'Muuu-umm.' The door swings wide open and the shock slices my breath in two.

'Off!' she rasps fiercely. 'Take that jumper off now.'

I take a step back. 'But I want to keep it on. I'm sorry about just now.'

She begins to tug at the sleeves. 'Ungrateful sod that

you are.' The sleeves stretch so far I'm afraid she'll pull them apart. 'You don't deserve this jumper,' she snarls.

'I had to get used to the idea. But I like it now.'

'Do you *want* me to hurt you?'

'Please let me keep it on.'

'You've been warned. Don't make me hurt you.'

I bend over so she can pull it over my head. The wool chafes my back.

'Now get out of my sight.' Clutching the jumper to her chest, she steps back into the bathroom.

I swallow.

'Didn't you hear what I said?'

'I'm sorry, Mum,' my voice quavers. 'I will put it on.'

'If you so much as touch it...'

I shrink back.

'Ssss,' she hisses, as if scaring off a rat in the shed. 'Get out of my house. Go on, piss off.'

27

With my bare feet stuffed into my boots and raincoat wide open, I run outside. Every breath is a big gulp of air. I barely feel the drizzle. Karl is standing by the rusty mooring post on the quay, loosening the last rope. His engine is running, the funnel behind the cabin already coughing smoke.

'I'm coming with you.' Before he can say anything, I've climbed on board.

'But I'm going to town.'

'I want to come, too.'

'Are you sure?'

'You're always saying...' I have to stop and gasp for breath, '... I can come along...'

'Of course.'

'Well, I want to come now.'

'Oh.'

'Please?'

He holds up a dented metal thermos flask and shakes it. 'Only enough coffee for one.'

'Water's fine.'

'I s'pose you didn't bring anything to eat with you.'

'Not really.'

'Counting on soft-touch Karl to see you right, as usual?'

'I don't need to eat anything.'

He talks like he couldn't care less, but I can tell he doesn't mind me tagging along.

'Please?'

'Okay,' he says, holding out his hand the way people do when they make a bet. 'You help me out today and I'll pay your food.' I slap his palm.

'I've got some crackers for you. And there's always plenty of fish on board.' He kicks a boot against the bow and the steel plate clangs.

'Get to work.' He hands me the loop of the hawser. 'Pull her on board and off we go.'

We're several yards offshore before I work up the nerve to look back at the house. At every window I'm expecting to see Mum's face looking back at me, but the whole place is dark. That scares me even more, cos I can still feel her eyes on me. Any second the door will fly open and she'll storm out screaming, her dressing gown flapping against her legs. It seems like forever before we clear the bay. I feel a little dizzy, as if I've been breathing in too much.

The house remains dark. The door stays closed.

It's a long time since I've seen our little island from this far away. Two lost and lonely houses: Karl's red with its pitch-black roof and ours white, half hidden behind a clutch of pine trees. From here, the hill behind our house hardly looks like a hill at all. A yellow burst of autumn hangs in the birch trees like slow-motion fireworks. We make a sharp turn at the red buoy; underwater, it's caked in barnacles and strands of seaweed. I'd always thought the top was painted, but now I see the white around the red light for what it is: a coat of gull shit.

We pass the cove and the rock I jumped from to go in after my ball. Since Dad disappeared, I've never gone swimming again. I'm too scared to go into the water, even close to shore where I can still see the pebbles and the sand beneath me, scared a hand might grab my ankle and drag me down into the deep. Besides, Mum threw my trunks on the fire and I won't go swimming bare-arsed.

Waves splash constantly against the bow but the boat is barely rolling. 'Come and stand in here,' shouts Karl, 'you'll get soaked out there!' The tip of the cigarette sticking out of the corner of his mouth has stopped glowing. He's leaning against the seat of the high chair, one hand on the wheel. Windscreen wipers squeak to and fro, trailing stripes across the glass but doing precious little to improve visibility. The small cabin smells of diesel and the walls are lined with the same brown panelling as Karl's kitchen and hallway.

'You're bleeding,' says Karl.

'Where?'

He points to my lower lip. 'Dab a bit of spit on it and it'll heal in no time.'

'I had a shave.'

'All part of the package, sonny. The rocky road to man-hood.'

I wipe my sleeve across my chin.

'Now all you're doing is spreading it about. Put some spit on it like I told you.'

I can't shake the image of Mum's burning eyes, her cruel mouth screaming but making no sound.

A blonde stares down at us from the calendar on the cab-in wall. Her legs are spread wide and she's lying in an enormous fishing net, wearing nothing but a pair of gold knickers and holding a breast in each hand as if she's trying to work out which one is heavier. Her breasts are rounder than Mum's. The nipples almost look like they've been stuck on, and they're pierced with shiny earrings. I try to look at her without attracting attention. I feel a warm glow rising deep in my belly.

'Not many of her calibre in Ladyville,' says Karl.

I try to look like I've been staring through the window off into the distance.

'That's a catch and a half on the calendar this month.'

'What are you on about?' I say as gruffly as possible.

'Don't try to kid me you haven't seen her, sonny.' He slaps me on the back. 'No man worth his salt could miss that.'

'Oh, that?'

'Yes, that.'

He begins to wipe the windows with a frayed dish-cloth. 'That heavy breathing of yours is getting the win-dows all steamed up.' He shoves the cloth into my hand. 'Wipe the rest, will you?'

'Fine.'

'Any hallos to pass on?'

'From who?'

'Your mother.'

'To you?'

'For example.'

'Not really.'

Karl grins. 'Well be sure and say hi from me when you get back home.'

A couple of gulls have been keeping us company ever since we left the island. One is balancing on the rail.

'Take over the wheel for a bit?'

'Which way do I steer her?'

'Straight ahead. Out here there's nothing for you to run into.' When I went into town with Dad ages ago, I was allowed to take the wheel for a while, too, but Dad stood behind me and held the bottom, just in case.

'Want some coffee?' asks Karl.

'Got enough for two, then?'

He purses his lips, nods, and takes down two beakers from a hatch above the windows. 'This beats sailing on my own, sonny. Always seems that much longer.'

I like it when he calls me 'sonny'. 'What time will we get there?'

'We've only just left.'

'Just so I know.'

'An hour or two, I reckon.'

'And then?'

'Pfff, unloading should take an hour. Then we'll take a look at the goodies on special offer this week.' He gives an oily laugh. 'After that we'll get some chow, and then it's back to the cutter.'

'Chow?'

'We have to eat something, don't we?' He puts a beaker of coffee down in front of me. Then he produces a crinkly packet of crackers and hands me a couple. 'These'll tide you over.'

At the first bite, the crackers splinter. Without a free hand to catch the crumbs, they spray down my jumper and onto the floor. Karl doesn't seem bothered.

'If you want some more, help yourself.'

'Cheers.'

'Already know what you want?'

'How d'you mean?'

'Later on.'

'These crackers will keep me going.'

'Ha ha ha, "crackers", he says. No lad, I'm talking about the ladies.'

I have to swallow a few times and focus on the expanse of waves.

'There's all sorts on offer.'

'I don't think I want one.'

'Wait till you see the selection.'

'I don't want one.'

He whacks me on the shoulder. 'Up to you. I'll not be footing the bill, at any rate.'

When rocks start to stick out of the water around us, Karl takes the wheel again. I crack my fingers, cramped from holding on so tightly. Steam stopped rising from my coffee a while back.

Spindly pine trees cling to some of the rocks. We pass a little island that's only big enough for a wooden cabin and a few birch trees alongside. Steps lead down to the water where a little motorboat is moored to two trees, fastened with different lengths of rope strung together. As we leave it behind us, the boat thumps against the rocks in our wake.

'Are we nearly there?' I shout over to Karl.

'A little over an hour.'

In the distance I can hear the wail of a chainsaw, but I

can't pinpoint where it's coming from.

On the next island, a dog comes running down from the cabin and stands there barking at us with its front paws in the water. Almost everyone passes straight by, so the daft mutt thinks it's his barking that's scared us off. Karl raises his hand to greet a skipper sailing toward us.

'Who's that?' I ask.

'No idea.'

'So why did you wave?'

'Everyone does.'

I don't have the nerve to wave at the next boat. And I only wave at the one after that when it's almost passed us. On the third boat, a boy on deck raises his hand without me doing anything; I copy him immediately. 'He put his hand up,' I say to Karl, and immediately hear how childish I sound. 'She's a decent catch, all right,' I say straight after, with a nod at the calendar girl.

'She is that,' replies Karl, taking his tobacco from his breast pocket. Leaning his belly against the wheel, he opens the pouch and takes a cigarette paper between his fingers.

'D'you want me to do it?'

He gawps at me in surprise.

'It was you that taught me.'

'Fine, if it makes you happy.'

'That way you can keep your hands on the wheel.'

'Go easy on the tobacco.'

I roll an almost-perfect cigarette, except there's not enough filling at the very ends.

'This one's yours.'

'Not bad at all.' He tilts his head toward me and opens his mouth.

'You look like a gull chick,' I say as I slot the cigarette

into the corner of his mouth. Karl gives a couple of shrill squawks and flicks on his lighter.

28

I thought when we got to Tramsund I'd see Brigitta herding a group of tourists over the quay, or Ingmar standing by his boat with a tower of groceries, or the policeman who came to see us that time. And everyone I didn't know would know about me, cos they'd've heard the story about my dad being lost at sea. But as we sail into the harbour, everything looks almost exactly the same as it did a few years ago. No one raises his hand to say hello.

'It's that green shed over there we want.' Karl points to a building and steers the cutter toward an empty space at the quayside. 'The fish market.'

Forklift trucks piled high with containers full of fish zip in and out of the sheds. A ramshackle lorry rattles past. Men in green overalls and wellies as long as their legs march around in all directions. No one looks our way. Boats along the quayside tug at their moorings, some ringed by oily rainbows that glisten on the water. There's so much to see, it makes me dizzy.

'See to the ropes!' Karl shouts at me. I sprint across the deck and do exactly as he tells me. It feels good to focus on something small. When I've tied all my knots, the sound of the engine dies away and the boat stops juddering.

'Get to it, sonny. This is where you earn them crackers.' Karl opens two hatches on the deck and disappears down the metal ladder. 'You stay on deck and stack everything I hand you up there on the quay.'

When the first containers appear, I'm standing ready to grab them and heave them ashore over the rail. But the more I get into the routine, the more my gaze wanders toward the quay.

'Eyes on the job, sonny.'

'Sorry.'

He hands me two more containers. Most of the ice that covered the fish has melted; it sloshes over my jeans and runs into my boots. It's freezing cold but I don't let on.

A man drives up to us in his forklift. Karl walks over to him. 'You can do the last few containers on your own,' he winks at me. 'I've got some talking to do.' He shakes hands with the forklift man. I can't follow what they're saying, but the man sounds a bit like Mum when she does her town talk. When our fish is on the quay, it takes the forklift man three trips to cart it all into the warehouse.

After a while he returns with some notes folded double and a few coins. 'Getting on for 480 kilos,' the man says. 'So that's just over three hundred.'

'No way that was 480 kilos,' Karl grumbles. 'Must've been six hundred at least.'

The forklift man shrugs. 'That was the lot. Even rounded it up in your favour.'

'Pack of swindlers.'

'The scales don't lie.'

'Heard that one before.'

'Take it or leave it.'

'Okay then, give me my three hundred plus.' He takes the money and stuffs it in his breast pocket without counting it. They say a gruff farewell, and the man climbs back on his forklift. Karl rolls a cigarette and hands the pouch to me without a second thought.

Out of nowhere a woman appears in front of us. Her long blonde hair fades to greyish brown at the roots. The skin under her eyes is bluish.

'Well, if it ain't our Badger,' she says. Her words sound like they've been shredded in the back of her throat.

Karl gives a broad smile. 'Looky here,' he says. 'Looky here.' He hitches up his overalls and scratches his neck. 'It's me all right. Yer very own bad penny.' Karl stretches out his arms to hug her but she dodges back. She's wearing big earrings and high-heeled boots.

'Come on, one little kiss,' he pleads in a weird, high-pitched voice.

'Oh no, you don't. I know better than to give a man like you a kiss for free.' When she leans forward, I can see the crack between her breasts.

'Ah go on, if you can't give *me* one...'

All of a sudden she points at me. 'Is this your boy?' They both look at me and I start to feel uncomfortable.

'Naah, you know I don't have a son.'

'So you're out with our Badger for the day?'

I keep my mouth shut cos I don't want her to hear how different my words sound from hers. I don't want her to laugh at me. Through her clothes I can see the breasts from the calendar.

'Tell me, lover boy. Are you going to be a fisherman, too?'

I look at the glowing tip of my cigarette and tap a few flakes of ash from it.

'Not much of a talker, is he?'

Karl bumps his fist against my shoulder.

'The boy barely knows he's alive.'

'Who is he, then?'

It annoys me that she doesn't know. 'I'm my father's son,' I say.

She eyes me up scornfully. 'Yes love, we all belong to daddy. Even if we don't always know what rock he's hiding under.'

'His dad drowned,' says Karl. The woman giggles. 'Straight up,' he continues. 'They never found a trace.'

'Jeezus,' says the woman. 'Ugh. That's a bit of a downer.'

'You're right, there. Damn right.'

I give them the angriest look I can muster.

'But he's a handsome lad,' says the woman. 'His dad must have been handsome, too.'

'Steady on,' says Karl. 'Got anything on offer for me today?'

'For you, Badger, always.'

If he had a tail, it would be wagging. 'Let's take a look, shall we,' he says, and climbs over the rail. 'Twenty?' he asks.

'Thirty-five. Standard rate, you know the score.'

The blonde woman walks a couple of paces ahead of him. Karl catches up and tries to put his arm round her. I climb off the boat and scurry after them.

'Thirty?' pleads Karl. 'Please?'

She giggles and pinches his backside. 'Thirty-five, Badger. And you know that's cheap as chips.'

'Okay, you win. Thirty-five.'

We're halfway across the quay when Karl turns around and glowers at me. 'Any closer and you'd be halfway up my arse.' My face turns bright red. 'Trailing after me like that. What are you, a dog?'

'Sorry.'

'You wait here for a bit.'

29

I wander across the quay, looking round every few steps to make sure I haven't lost sight of the cutter. Karl has disappeared behind the warehouses. None of the boats moored here are Ingmar's. I find a corner where I can keep my eye on the esplanade as well as the cutter and sit down on a big concrete block. I scrape crusty splinters from the rusted ring that's anchored in the middle. Blood wells up under my fingernail.

I recognize the place from when I was here with Dad. Not the green warehouses of the fish market, but the buildings and houses wedged up against one another and the narrow streets that disappear between them. Nothing looks as tall as I remember. Though it's still afternoon, the lamps hanging from cables above the road are already on. The part of town I walked through with Dad must be somewhere in among these streets. The buses haven't changed at all, clunking and groaning their way through the traffic.

Every time I hear the buzz of a scooter, I think it must be Ingmar. He'd be difficult to pick out cos all the boys have short hair. Some have a moustache. Most of the scooters have a girl perched on the back, hood up and blonde hair fluttering.

There are more kinds of gulls flying around here than back on the island. Some are speckled brown, and there are those ones that have a black helmet and a fiery red beak.

I think of my gulls locked in Miss Augusta's bedroom, and it dawns on me that if I never went home, they'd starve. I fed them yesterday and I'll feed them again tomorrow, but the thought that no one knows they're locked up in there gives me the jitters.

Further along, down the side of one of the warehouses, I see a small telephone box. It's odd to think I could call Mum from here. I've never spoken to her on the phone. She'd pick up the receiver and say, 'Hello, Dora Hammermann speaking,' in her best town talk. And then I'd have to say something back.

Mum would be quiet for a while. Then I could say something like, 'My gull is locked in Miss Augusta's bedroom.' But perhaps she'd go over there and let them out and then I wouldn't be able to take care of them anymore. Just as well I don't have any money with me, so I don't have to think about it, though I could always ask Karl to lend me some. Then I'd be able to tell her I was in Tramsund and that I was sorry about the jumper. And she could say it was all okay and ask me when I was coming home.

'This evening. No need to wait up.'

If only I'd put on that jumper this morning, nothing would be the matter. We'd be sitting across from each another right now at the kitchen table. Maybe she'd fetch the toilet bag with the scissors and the trimmer and cut my hair. I'd take my jumper off and sit in the middle of the kitchen with a cool white sheet draped over me. She'd fill the plant sprayer with cold water to dampen my hair and give me a sneaky squirt in the neck, just for a laugh.

30

'Over here,' says Karl.

We go into a small building with steamed-up windows. Tube lighting hangs from the ceiling above the tables. I tag along behind him, but not close enough to look like a dog.

'Hungry?' Karl asks.

'Pretty hungry.'

'Grub for two,' he says to the boy behind the counter, who spreads two sheets of newspaper side by side and starts piling food onto them. He looks a bit like Ingmar, too.

Meanwhile Karl grabbles in his overalls for some coins. He counts them out on his hand, turns one over, and grabbles for more. He ends up handing over a note.

Karl seems angry with me. I want to say something to him about the woman with the crack between her breasts, but I'm not sure what. I sit down at an empty table and try to pull in my chair, but it's nailed to the floor. At the other tables, men are leaning over the pile of food on their newspaper. They've all hooked a protective arm around their meal, forking it into their mouth with the other hand. They're eating the same as us: deep-fried fish, boiled potatoes, and cauliflower, which is white, not grey like when Mum makes it. The grease from the fish leaves dark stains on the newspaper.

Karl takes off his woolly hat. So this is what someone looks like when they've just had sex. You can't really see any difference. 'Stop staring at me like that, sonny.'

'I'm not staring.'

'Then what's the matter?'

'Nothing.'

We fork away at our food.

'Why are you called Badger?'

Karl grins. 'That's between me and the ladies.'

The newspaper leaves inky smudges on my cauliflower. The fish tastes best. Karl eats his potatoes first, then his cauliflower, and saves the fish till last. His lips flap open and shut every time he chews. Every few mouthfuls he sprinkles salt over everything. I copy him.

The plastic clock above the door says it's nearly half past three. Karl clears his newspaper before I do. He scrunches it into a big ball, leans back in his chair, and lets out an almighty burp. No one around us even raises an eyebrow. 'Get that food down you, lad. If we're going to make it home, it's time we got back to the cutter.' He runs his tongue over his teeth to dislodge bits of food and then starts rolling a cigarette. 'You too?'

I nod.

'Rolling your own, I s'pose?'

'Yeah,' I say through a mouthful of cauliflower.

He tosses the pouch onto the table. 'At this rate, my baccy will be gone in no time.'

The bell above the door rings and a woman walks in, eyebrows bunched low. Her hair is scraped back over her scalp and her pointy nose sticks out like a beak. It's not raining, but everything about her looks bedraggled.

'A woman,' I say to Karl. He turns toward the door and then back to face me.

'Yeah. Well, they can't all be calendar girls.'

31

The journey back goes much quicker than I expected. From the rear deck I can still see the town for a while. The more islands we sail past, the fewer the houses. Before I know it, we've reached the little island with the dog. It charges down into the water and starts barking at us again. After that it's just rocks with the odd tree, then nothing but empty sea.

The cabin radio is broadcasting the station we sometimes listen to at home. The longer we sail, the more something starts gnawing away at my stomach. A hungry ache, the kind that doesn't disappear when you eat something. I let out a couple of heavy sighs—it doesn't help. Karl offers me a cigarette but I don't feel like one. We don't say a word the whole way back. The early evening settles in around us.

32

Snowflakes swarm around the lamp, so light they could easily drift back up into the night sky. When we reach the island, Karl turns on the searchlight on the cabin roof so he can see the bay.

Our house is dark. The rustling of trees is the only sound from the shadows. The deck is slippery. Before Karl can say a word, I'm at the bow of the boat with the rope in my hands, ready to tie her up to the quay.

'Well, that was quite an adventure, sonny.' Karl brings his hand down on my shoulder and then shuffles off home. 'I'll need some fish sorting in a few days' time, if you're up for it.'

'Great,' I answer.

I hear him spit and watch the dark absorb his silhouette.

'Sleep tight,' I call after him, but he can't hear me anymore. His front door squeaks, then slams shut. A window lights up.

I was hoping our door would be locked so I'd have to spend the night outside. Then I could go and sleep at

Miss Augusta's with my gull chick. Or I could knock on Karl's door and tell him Mum locked me out by mistake, and ask if he'd let me sleep on his settee. But the kitchen door opens, as usual.

I can't bring myself to turn on the light, so I feel my way through the kitchen and up to my room. The house holds its breath, and even my slightest movement seems to make a racket. I skip brushing my teeth, slurp some water from the tap, and take a blind piss in the washbasin before crawling into bed with all my clothes on.

There's a yellowish glow on the horizon. I imagine it's the lights of Tramsund, though I know it must be the moon behind the clouds.

33

A wad of paper is floating in the yellow water. Mum never flushes the toilet when she's trying to avoid me. She moves through the house without making a sound, so as not to give herself away.

I empty the laundry basket but I can't find Dad's jumper with the anchor on it. It's not in the cupboard or in the rubbish bin. I don't have the nerve to put on another jumper.

I hear something clatter on the draining board and sneak downstairs. The dress she's wearing is way too flimsy. The straps dig into her shoulders and I can see goose pimples on her back. Plastic pearls are hanging from her ears.

'Mum?' She jumps but goes on ignoring me. Picking

up her bowl of porridge, she goes and sits in the arm-chair in the living room. 'Do you know where Dad's jumper is?' Before I reach her, she's heading for the kitch-en again. 'I'm sorry about yesterday. I want to put on the jumper you gave me.' Now she's halfway up the stairs. 'Please, Mum?'

'Don't. Call. Me. That.' She motions as if to throw the bowl at me. A splodge of porridge falls on the stair below her. 'I have a name.'

'Dora,' I say. It sounds strange and new, coming from my mouth.

'That's what you call me from now on. And don't keep traipsing around after me.'

'I really want to wear the jumper with the anchor.'

'Too bad. It's not yours.'

34

I lay a trail of chewed-up mussels leading from the bed to my lap, and sit under the window with my back against the wall, waiting for my chick to appear. 'I've pissed my mum off and now she's avoiding me,' I mumble at the rustling under the bed. 'Yesterday I went to Tramsund and back with Karl. I've been there before with Dad, but that was a long time ago.'

Rain beats against the window and gurgles down the blocked gutter. The beams of the house brace themselves with every gust of wind. 'Karl's my friend, I think.'

The room is a mess, strewn with dark shell fragments. The picked-clean bones of a dried fish are scattered on the quilt around the container of macaroni, with its brown rim of dried tomato sauce. The sauce has splattered everywhere, even as far as the door. 'Your mother's a mean one.' Out on the landing I can hear the tick of mussel shells as she tries to crack them open.

Little Gull comes out from under the bed and waddles warily toward me. He seems to have grown. His head and body are more in proportion, and a hook is taking shape at the end of his beak. He barely manages to eat any of the mussel gunk I've put on the floor and ends up smearing most of it across the floorboards under his feet. I take a little between my fingers to feed him. Convinced I don't mean him any harm, he comes closer. He potters around me, grabs the cord on my raincoat, and pulls it. Then he tries to climb up my leg. 'Easy does it, Little Gull. You still shouldn't smell too much like me.'

With my little finger under his backside, I help him onto my lap. His legs kick nervously as they leave the floor, and his feet take an uncertain hold on my jeans. I stretch out my hands on either side of him, ready to steady him if he falls over. It tickles when he tries to pick at the legs of my jeans. He snaps cheekily at the shiny metal of my zip. 'Stop it. That's weird!' I hold a smidgen of chewed-up mussel over his head. 'Here, eat this.'

'Mum wanted me to put on that jumper of Dad's, but I wouldn't. And now I can't find it anywhere.'

My chick yawns. I didn't even know gulls could do that. A shiver runs through his little body and he shakes his stumpy wings. Thin films slide open and shut in front of his eyes. 'Look, Little Gull, here's some more sick for you.' I chuckle, and he nearly slides off my lap.

Eventually he begins to settle down, folds his legs, and turns his head to bury his beak in the down on his back. The films in front of his eyes go up and down more slowly till his left eye closes and his right becomes a watchful peephole. I want to stroke him but stop myself just in time. I look on, motionless. There's no sign at all that his little heart is still beating. You can't even tell he's breathing.

After a while my right leg goes to sleep. Cautiously, I try to bend my knee. Little Gull starts up with a peep. 'Easy now, easy.' Before he falls off, I put him down on the floor. He disappears under the bed in a second, leaving a shit stain on my jeans.

35

The kitchen window is all steamed up so I can't see inside. The radio is on and there's a bitter smell of coffee. The kitchen door won't open wide enough to let me in. Something's been pushed up against it. 'Mum?'
She doesn't answer.
'Dora?'
'Yes.'
'Can I come in?'
'What for?'
'I've cut my finger and I need a plaster.'
'Just stay out there for a minute,' she says, as if she's preparing a surprise for me.
'What are you doing in there?'
'We've got company.'
'Company?'
'I've invited someone over.'
Who else can it be but Karl?
'Our neighbour's here.'

'Hello there, Young Master Hammermann.'

'How come he's "our neighbour" all of a sudden?'

'What else do you want me to call him?'

'His name's Karl.'

Her face appears in the gap beside the door. She holds up the scissors and snips a few times.

'Your mother's smartening me up,' booms Karl. 'High time, she reckoned.'

I push against the door and the table moves a little. 'Now, don't make trouble. We were having a grand old time till you showed up.'

'But I can come in, can't I?'

'I'd rather you didn't,' she says, and goes back to cutting Karl's hair.

I want to go up to my room but I can't resist the urge to worm my head around the side of the door. Karl is sitting bare-chested on a kitchen chair with his back to me. A couple of gingery hairs curl from his freckled shoulders. He's waving his arms around and talking up a storm about a recent catch, tossing in a joke for good measure. They don't notice me watching them. Mum is standing behind him, shuffling from side to side. She takes locks of his hair between her fingers and snips off the ends. Then she ruffles his mop of hair and blows loose tufts from his neck. Karl giggles and says it tickles. 'Sit still,' she says. He doesn't obey straight off and she jabs his fat shoulder with the scissors.

'Ow!' Karl shrinks away from her. 'What do you think you're doing?'

'Sorry,' she says. 'You moved and my hand slipped.'

'You stabbed me!'

There's a red dot on his shoulder.

'No need to make a song and dance. You're a man, aren't you?'

His fingers feel for the red dot. Mum raps his knuckles with the scissors. 'Leave it alone. We don't want that nasty blood of yours smeared all over the place.'

She takes the hair trimmer from the blue toilet bag that contains our haircut stuff. The flex isn't long enough to stretch from the socket to where Karl is sitting. 'Shift your chair over here, will you. That way I can shave your neck.'

Karl sits back down and lowers his chin to his chest. Mum runs a bald stripe up his neck and a little moustache of hair forms along the teeth of the trimmer. She gives it a shake and the moustache floats to the floor. Karl tries to say something but he can't be heard above the buzzing. He must think it's funny, cos his chest and shoulders wobble. Mum takes a step back, admires her work, and clicks off the trimmer.

'You've got thick hair.'

'Is that good or bad?'

'Thick, that's all.' She wipes his neck with the tea towel and hangs it back on its hook. In a deadpan voice, she says 'We've got ourselves a peeping Tom, Karl.' They both turn to look at me. Startled, I yank my head back and bang my jaw on the side of the door. The kitchen echoes with laughter.

36

Branches. Pine cones. I kick everything out of the way, stamp on saplings and toadstools. I only hold back when I come across big rocks, so I don't break the bones in my foot. Miss Augusta's front door opens outward but I keep on kicking till it cracks into planks that fall into the hallway.

Gull does what she always does. Little Gull is hungry again. It hasn't even been half an hour since I fed them last, and already they've forgotten. I pull the door shut again—stupid birds.

I take a couple of floorboards from the living room and break them across my knee, nudging the splinters into a pile with the toe of my boot. I tear a few pages from a bloated book that's dried up again and stuff them into the little stove in the corner of the kitchen, along with the broken bits of wood. Five matches later it catches fire. I lie down under the table and gaze up at the stars in the wooden sky, constellations I drew there in pencil long ago.

37

It's Ingmar at the wheel. He sails into the bay faster than his dad used to. He takes the turn too wide, and the steel of the red bow scrapes along the concrete of the quay. I give it a push to fend it off but that hardly makes any difference. A dog jumps up, barking. Its claws scratch the edge of the rail. I'm glad Ingmar is too busy sorting things out in the cabin to see me jump. 'You took the turn too wide!' I shout.

'Dog!' yells Ingmar when the sound of the engine dies down. The mutt stops barking immediately. Ingmar hooks a finger inside the collar of his jumper and jiggles it up and down. He's wearing his dad's cap. It sits low on his forehead and makes him look stern.

'Stroke him behind the ears and he'll settle down.' A fishy fug comes from the dog's muzzle. Its tongue is a limp flap of ham.

'You've got to let him get a sniff at you first.' The dog snuffles my hand till it's wet and licks between my fingers. 'He likes you,' says Ingmar. 'Now you can stroke him.' I'm not keen, but I do it anyway. The mutt gives a little growl. His eyes are so black, I can't tell the pupil from the rest.

'Call that stroking?'

'Huh?'

'Looks more like you're dusting him off. That's how my girlfriend does it.'

'I don't know that many dogs.'

'Scratch his head. He loves that.' In among the rough grey coat I can feel a couple of ticks, some as big as peas, others smaller, as if he has cat's nipples behind his ears. I pull my hand back, but as soon as I do, the dog bumps his nose against it and licks my palm. 'Now you have to keep stroking him forever or he'll bite you to death.'

For a second I believe Ingmar.

'Just kidding, of course.'

''Course.' I slide my hands into my pockets just in case.

'Are you the boss now?'

'You could say that, yeah.' Ingmar nods like he doesn't care, but I can see in his eyes that he's proud of himself.

'You still have to learn to steer. That turn into the bay was a bit dodgy.'

'It's this quay. I don't have trouble anywhere else, you know.'

He has a little nick on his chin.

'I've had a shave, too.'

'Huh?'

I point at his chin.

'Old razor blades.'

'I had the same thing.'

Ingmar holds out his hand. 'Got a list for me?' He takes the envelope from me, tears it open, and mumbles his way through our order under his breath. 'As long as there's no funny fruit on it.' He tries to say the words like they're his own, but they're as much his dad's as the mumbling routine with the list.

'I was in Tramsud the other day.'

'Oh,' he says, without looking up.

'Were you there, too?'

'What day was it?'

'Six days ago.'

'Might have been,' he says.

'With Karl, you know, from next door. We had to start back at four.'

The dog paces around Ingmar and sweeps its wagging tail against his calves. Then it tries to leap up at him. 'Down,' Ingmar snarls. 'Down.' Hanging its head, the dog toddles over to the cabin and lies down with its back to us.

'He does as he's told.'

'As long as you're the one that feeds them, you can teach animals anything.'

'I've trained a gull.'

'You've what?'

'Same thing you've done with your dog.'

'Can you do that with a gull?'

'Not so as it does what it's told. Not yet. But he lets me feed him and he sits on my lap. He'll soon be my little gull.'

'Your little gull?'

'Want to come and see him?'

Ingmar laughs. 'No time for that.'

'It won't take long.' The idea that I have something to show him almost makes me feel light-headed. My own little gull! I can show him how I lure the mother out of the room. I can teach Ingmar how to disappear.

'I can show you right now if you want. I keep him in the house over the other side of the island.'

'I've got to get on.' Ingmar folds the list and slips it into his breast pocket.

'Or would you like some coffee?'

He shakes his head.

'It's no trouble.'

'Maybe another time.'

'Next time?'

'Maybe.'

'I'll have it ready for you coming.'

'We'll see.'

'Up to you.'

'Cheerio.' He taps the side of his cap with his finger. 'See you in a fortnight.'

'Cheerio,' I echo. His dog barks and snaps at a low-flying gull.

38

In the morning there's a knock on my bedroom door. I'm still only half awake. 'Yeah?'

'It's me.'

'I know.'

'Open up.'

'Hang on.'

I get out of bed and pull on my underpants.

'Are you going to open that door?'

'Just a sec.'

I quickly pull on my jeans and open the door. A towel

is twisted around her wet hair. Other than that, she's naked. I swallow uneasily. Her breasts are not the half moons they used to be. Her nipples still point straight ahead, but now they're less like hard pellets and more like raisins. 'Get your brush.'

'Why?'

'Because I'm asking you to.'

'Is yours broken?'

'I want you to brush my hair.'

She unwinds the towel around her head and begins to dry her hair. Her upper arms are sinewy. Her breasts wobble. I try not to look.

'Shouldn't you put on some clothes first?'

'No, I'm fine.' She tosses her hair back.

'But it's much too cold.'

'No, it's not.'

'You can't walk around the house like that.'

'Like what?'

'You know... all naked like that.'

'Who's going to object? Karl?' She turns and goes downstairs, humming to herself. The last time I saw her naked was years ago, when she used to lie on the rusty lounger so the summer sun would turn her skin red. It was during one of those summers I first noticed that the triangle of dark curls between Mum's legs concealed a little mouth, two vertical lips with the tip of a cat's tongue sticking out between them. 'Stop spying on your mother like that,' she said, and turned over onto her stomach. The seams of the lounger were imprinted on her back and behind. Little black hairs peeped out between her buttocks, a dark furrow of wiry grass. I tried to pluck one. 'Ow!' She clenched her buttocks and slapped the back of my hand.

Then she giggled.

Mum is sitting on a chair in the kitchen, knees tucked under her chin and breasts pressed flat against her legs. The skin from her neck to her breasts is puckered with tiny wrinkles, like limp lettuce. The pair of knickers she's pulled from the drying rack is digging into her hips. Her hair is still dark from the shower. I've brought down her dressing gown and drape it over her shoulders. 'Here, put this on.'

'I don't want it.' She flings the dressing gown in the direction of the sideboard. The vase on top wobbles precariously and only just stays upright. 'Now brush my hair.'

'I don't know how.' I try to give her the brush.

'Don't make such a fuss.'

Hesitantly, I take a length of her hair between my fingers and carefully stroke the brush through the ends. Drops of water fall on the floor. Little by little, I move up from the ends and she bows her head slightly. Suddenly she grabs my hand, steers it to the curve where her neck meets her shoulder, and presses my palm against her skin. 'To brush properly you have to touch me.'

Her skin feels warm. I edge my hand away from her neck slightly.

'You need to be rougher,' she says.

'I'm doing my best.'

I run the brush down from the crown of her head in long strokes and it catches in a knot of hair. 'Pull,' she says. I take a firm hold of the hair above the knot, as if squeezing it hard will numb the pain, and then tug with the brush.

'Ow,' she moans.

'You wanted me to pull, didn't you?' I dangle the loose knot of hair in front of her face, like a dead baby mouse held up by its tail.

Even though it looks like I'm finished, I continue to let the brush glide though her hair. Carefully, I rub the bristles into the hollow of her neck. The little blonde hairs on her arm stand on end.

'I think I'm finished.'

She runs her hands through her hair.

'Now plait it.'

'How?'

She takes a purple rubber band from around her wrist. 'Tell me when you need this.'

The plait goes squinty. I untwine it and divide her hair into three new strands. Before I can ask, she hands me the rubber band and I wind it round the end of the plait. 'It's not all that good,' I say.

She gets up and goes into the toilet to look at herself in the mirror. 'You're right,' she smiles and shakes her hair loose, then twists it neatly into a bun, looking at me in the mirror all the while. 'There's nothing you can't learn. We've got all the time in the world.'

39

The crackle of wood is coming from the round stove in the corner. All that's missing now is the smell of coffee. 'That was *my* chair,' I say. Little Gull flounders across the kitchen table and only has eyes for the biscuits I've crumbled on the tabletop. 'Miss Augusta always sat on that chair there. It's her bed you hatched in. And that's where my dad used to sit.'

Every now and then my chick manages to pick up some of the crumbs, but I still have to feed him most of them. I take a piece of biscuit I've softened by sucking on it, and hold it just out of reach above my chick's head. He taps greedily against the red button on my cuff, opens his beak, and waits. I wait, too, just to tease him.

His cry of hunger sounds a little off-key—half gull, half chick. 'Easy now, easy,' I murmur gently and push the biscuit into his little beak. He swallows it instantly. 'Crikey. You're allowed to taste it on the way down, you know.'

I look on as he tries to eat a piece of biscuit that's already fallen out of his beak a few times. He's able to pick it up okay, but when he straightens up and opens his beak to swallow, it keeps falling back onto the table. He tries again and again. Eventually he gives up and scrambles further across the table, only to come across the same piece of biscuit again a little while later.

'This table wasn't only made for eating at. That's what Miss Augusta said. You know what that means?' I chuckle. ''Course you don't.' The thought starts my cock tingling and makes me feel bashful in front of my gull chick, especially knowing it was old Miss Augusta and fat Karl on the table. I try not to think about it.

'Maybe you can come and live in our shed. I can make a birdhouse for you and you can fly back there every evening. I'll think of a name and teach it to you, and then you can come flying when I call. Till then you'll have to stay here with your own mother so she can watch over you.'

Slowly but surely the down on his back is beginning to make way for feathers, same on his wings. He shakes his backside and deposits a white squirt of shit on the table. I get up and fetch the dried-out dishcloth that's draped over the tap. Little Gull snaps at it as I wipe away the stain. 'That's not for eating!' He keeps on trying anyway.

'Karl says Mum's a woman who's all alone, but she's got me. I'm enough for her. She doesn't want me talking too much to other people.'

My chick's eyelids are almost oval, which makes his eyes look a little bit human. They'll change as he grows and become just as round as his mother's. I'm glad that won't happen for a while yet. 'Eventually your mother will leave you behind. She'll fly away and then you'll have to fend for yourself.' I put some crumbs on the tip of my tongue and stick it so far out that it starts to hurt at the root. It takes a while for my chick to catch on. With my chin on the table, I wait till he plucks up enough courage to come closer. He steps toward me, pecking at crumbs that aren't there, pausing every few seconds and watching timidly till he's inches from my face. We look straight at one another. His black eyes are unfathomably deep. Words pound in my head—don't jump, don't jump—knowing he's about to snatch the wet crumbs from my tongue any moment now. Slowly he cranes his neck and tilts his head slightly.

His beak flashes forward and pecks my nose. I jolt my head back, and Little Gull jumps in fright and tumbles backward. It really only tickled. 'Sorry,' I say softly as he waddles away.

'You'll be a sky sailor one day,' I whisper. 'My dad would think so, too.' I rest my arm on the back of the chair next to me. 'He always used to sit here, but you know that already.'

40

We take shelter behind the cooling shed. The cold is nipping at my ears. 'Stiff old wind. Coming from the north,' Karl says, waving his tobacco.

'I'll pass.'

'Young Master Hammermann turning down ciggies? I'm not charging, you know.'

'Stop calling me that.'

'Dearie me. Young sir got the hump today?'

'My name's not "young sir", either.'

'Well, that mother of yours is a damn sight cheerier, let me tell you.' He stretches a cigarette paper between his fingers. 'I might be wrong, but she seems to be taking a bit of a shine to me, don't you reckon?'

I shrug my shoulders.

'Does she ever talk about me?'

'Not really.'

'We had a right old laugh together in that kitchen of yours the other day.'

'Can't you find a barber's in Tramsund?'

'And pay for the privilege? Not likely. Your mother does a good enough job. And it was needing a trim.' Karl takes off his woolly hat and shows me the result. 'Cut off enough to stuff a goose.'

The wind blasts tiny splinters of ice into my face. They prick like needles.

'You know my style with the ladies—let 'em take their own sweet time,' Karl grins. 'I only come when I'm invited.' He turns his back to me cos his lighter keeps blowing out. 'And your mother's no ugly duckling. I've always thought that. Not had too many kids. That way they keep their figure.' He whacks me on the shoulder. 'Say what you like, but I know enough about the ladies to know she likes me.' He takes a couple of steps forward, looks in the direction of our house, and then steps back again.

'You should leave her alone.'

'Easy does it.' He raises his hands in the air. 'She's the one making nice with me, not the other way round. Besides, it's just the two of us here, three counting you. So we'd best make a go of it together.'

'She wants nothing to do with you.'

'No? Then why did she give me this?' He clamps his cigarette in the corner of his mouth and zips open his raincoat. 'Smart, eh?'

Karl is wearing Dad's shirt, the one with the blue stitches down the sides. It gapes open between the buttons, exposing the hair on his belly.

'Brought over a whole bag of stuff, so she did.' He looks down at himself. 'Some are a bit on the tight side but eh...' He slaps his belly with both hands. 'Won't take me long to stretch 'em out a bit.'

Dad's shirt. Dad's shirt. Dad's shirt stretched over that pasty back of his, with its cauliflower freckles, a back so lumpy you can't even see his shoulder blades.

'Enough of yer dirty looks, sonny.' He thumps my shoulder. Glowing ash from his cigarette falls on the shirt. He notices too late, and though he brushes it off with his fat fingers, it leaves a brown speck. 'See. It's already starting to look more like mine.' My nails dig into my palms. Karl zips up his coat. Dad's shirt. The words pulse through my head. Dad's shirt. I feel my whole body tense and I spit. It lands on his leg. Karl stares down at the slimy trail in surprise. 'So now you think you can spit on me?'

'Hands off,' I growl. 'They're not your clothes.' I spit again, aiming for his face this time but it hits his chest. 'And keep away from my mum, you fat bastard.'

Karl's mouth hangs open a little, air hisses between his teeth and turns to laughter. It rolls from his mouth, growing louder and louder. 'Bastard? Me? Says the good for nothin' that eats my fish and scrounges my ciggies. And now he thinks he can use me for target practice.' He roars louder. 'No wonder yer mother wants the company of a real man once in a while.'

I run for home. Karl's bellowing follows me all the way to the front door. I bound up to my room two stairs at a time and pull open Dad's wardrobe. It's worse than I thought. All the shelves are empty, drawers too. There's a hollow sound as I slam it shut.

'What have you done?' I scream through the house.

A door opens upstairs.

'No need to yell.'

'Where are Dad's clothes?'

'What do you mean?'

'Karl's wearing his shirt. He says you took him over a whole bag.'

'I decided to have a bit of a clear-out.'

'A clear-out?'

'Well, you didn't want them, did you?'

'But Karl is wearing his white shirt.'

'And now *you* want it, all of a sudden?'

'It's Dad's. You should've kept your hands off it.'

'If you want it that bad, you can go over there and get it back yourself.'

41

I have to wait till the next afternoon before Karl finally takes the boat out again. All morning I kept peering out from behind the curtains to check whether he'd gone. And suddenly he had.

His kitchen table is stained and specked with burn marks. Four peach halves are lying in a pool of juice in a greasy bowl. The tube light above the sink is still on. I hold my breath so I can hear the sounds of the house better. The stuffed gulls and ducks on the shelf above the door stare at me through the holes where their eyes should be. Bright yellow strips of flypaper are crusted black with dried-up bugs.

There's not much in his living room: a small television on a table in the corner, a small settee and three leather chairs crowded around a coffee table. Wherever he sits, Karl is always facing an empty chair. Nothing much has changed since the days when I used to sneak over and watch TV when he wasn't home. Endless repeats of the news. I couldn't follow what they were saying, but there were always exciting pictures of a fire or a car crash to keep me watching over and over. Once in a while there'd be a cowboy film.

I only came here when I knew for sure he was out fishing. I used to fill his teapot and water the plant by the window. Now it's grown into a stringy shrub that sprawls across the pane. Its brown leaves crumble in my hand.

The dark TV screen shows me my reflection creeping through the room. There's no rubbish bag full of clothes anywhere. I open the cupboard under the stairs, releasing a damp and mouldy stink, and accidentally knock over a line-up of clinking bottles with my foot. I grope for the light switch, and the bulb hanging from the ceiling shines bare and bright. Greasy jars of boned fish line the shelves against the wall, blackcurrant jam labels still stuck to the glass. The rest of the shelves are stacked with the same tinned veg as at our house.

I never used to go upstairs for fear there would be no time to escape if Karl came home without warning. Even now I scan the quay before setting foot on the stairs.

The sheet on his bed has been kicked aside. The white pillowcase bears the faint brown imprint of his greasy hair. I open his wardrobe. There's not much in there, and none of it belongs to Dad. A tangle of overalls, discarded socks and shirts lies beside his bed. I turn it over with my foot, but there's nothing that's Dad's.

A small photo, framed and yellowed, hangs above his bed. The figure on the left is Karl, or a version of Karl that's shrunk in the wash. He must have been around fifteen, looking awkward in a jacket, shoulders bunched up and hair scraped into a side parting. His eyes are fixed on something just below the lens. The man next to him has the same rough-hewn head as Karl, and is looking straight at me. Of the two of them, he looks more like Karl does now. Father and son have the same neat parting. The jacket Karl's father is wearing is still hanging in the wardrobe.

A black-and-white passport photo is tucked into the corner of the frame. It's of a young woman, looking sidelong at the photographer. She seems a little surprised, as if she's just glanced up to see who's called her name, and the beginnings of a smile are hovering around her lips. Her curls have been tugged back into a plait, her cheeks are white as candle wax. The only resemblance to Karl is in her eyes.

I hold my breath for a moment, thinking I hear the drone of Karl's engine, but the sound disappears. The trapdoor that leads to the attic is open, and lures me up into a dark space where a single square of light falls through a small window. My eyes have to adjust to the gloom. Dust floats in the air. Washing lines are strung across the attic; socks and tea towels have been hung up to dry. Further back, old wooden gardening tools lie in the half-light and a tall cupboard rises up against the back wall like a giant tombstone. There are cobwebs everywhere, piles of planks, a dead mouse I only discover when I tread on it. No bag of clothes. I step around the open trapdoor and peer into the darker half of the attic. Something is right there in front of me, but I can't tell what. I look closer and almost tumble through the trapdoor in terror. A dark silhouette is hanging from one of the beams, legless. It sways slowly in the draught, half a man hanging by the neck.

It's the jacket of Dad's best suit, draped over a coat hanger. The trousers have slid onto the floor. At home it hung at the back of the wardrobe with the winter coats. I can't remember him ever wearing it.

Now that I have proof Mum really has given Dad's clothes to Karl, I'm even more pissed off I can't find them. I climb down the ladder and charge through the house. I search the bathroom, the kitchen, and take another look in the living room. Nothing. I rush back up to the bedroom, shove the chairs aside, and turn over the tangle of dirty washing again. I get down on my knees and discover a rubbish bag under the bed. I pull it out and see Dad's trousers, shirts, and jumpers, even his rolled-up socks and underpants, all stuffed in carelessly. At the bottom are his heavy work shoes and his smart pair. The leather on the inside is dark and hard. Dad's foot has rubbed away the gold letters on the insole, and the heels are worn down at one corner. Immediately I picture how his knees always pointed out slightly as he walked, the bounce in his step.

Mum has been thorough. She's even given away his watch and sunglasses. I get Dad's best suit from the attic and stuff it into the bag along with the rest of his things, checking under the bed to make sure I haven't missed anything. I spot a little box up at the far end and pull it out. It takes me a while to figure out where I've seen it before. It was the box that always stood on Miss Augusta's bedside table. The hinges open without a squeak to reveal all kinds of things: tangled earrings, the necklace of blue stones—far less blue than my memory of it. At the bottom there's a tattered, well-thumbed Bible, and a postcard of a church. *Dear Pernille, You asked me to send you a card. Here it is. I haven't seen the church in the photograph but it's called the Sacred Heart. I'll be back this afternoon. Your Karl.* In the place where the address goes there's only the letter *P.* followed by the words *My boat beats the postman any day.*

The box also contains a pile of photos of Miss Augusta, held together by a crumbling rubber band. All the pictures are from the time before she was like a grandma. The year is scribbled in pencil on the back of each photo, along with short descriptions in Karl's handwriting: *P. as a little girl at the seaside, P. in Tramsund, P. with parents.* There's one photo where I can't recognize Miss Augusta straight off, though there are only two people in it. A woman is sitting on a bench, her wrists crossed, her hands perched on one knee. Beside her, a few feet away, is the man from the photo above Karl's bed. *Pernille and Father* is scrawled on the back.

I return the photos to the box and slide it back under the bed.

42

Every time the wind rattles our house, I think it's Karl coming to get me back for spitting at him. By now he must have realized I've been over at his place.

It's the following afternoon, and Karl has been watching TV all morning. I can tell cos he always watches with the curtains closed.

Mum is keeping to herself up in her bedroom. I want to let her know I've rescued Dad's things, but I don't know how. His clothes are back in their old familiar piles in his wardrobe. Only the white shirt with the blue stitching is missing. Karl can keep that. After the other day, it'd only remind me of him anyway.

43

'I'll take you down to the kitchen in a bit.' Little Gull is sitting on my lap, snapping wet bread from between my fingers. 'Karl had Dad's clothes, but I went over and got them back.'

Out on the landing, Gull has been quiet for a while, but suddenly she's wailing like a siren. I hear footsteps rushing up the stairs. My body stiffens. They walk into the bathroom and back out again, then the bedroom door swings open. Little Gull dives from my lap and escapes under the bed.

'Mum?' I swallow. 'Dora?'

'I thought you were dead,' she says. 'But you're here.' Two steps and she's standing beside me. I haul myself out of the chair.

There's blood and grime under her fingernails, smears of dirt on her cheeks and forehead. Dark rings suck her eyes deeper in their sockets, so deep I can see the outline of her skull.

'I looked all over for you.' She flings her arms round me and squeezes like an inflatable ring that's been pumped up too tight. 'And then I thought of this dump.'

'I'm not dead.'

'I knew it.'

'You don't need to be afraid.'

Tears well in the corners of her eyes. 'Avoiding me is worse,' she sniffs. 'You do that on purpose. You don't want me.'

'Of course I do.' I try to wriggle free of her. 'I've not been here long.'

'Why do you come here?'

'No reason. Sometimes I come looking for a present for you,' I stammer.

'You should be with me.' She clasps her cold, rough hands to my cheeks. 'I should be all you need.'

'You are. You know that.'

Suddenly she squeezes my cheeks so tight my jaw drops like a fish's. 'What was that on your lap?'

'Nothing.' I try to avoid her stare and focus on the mole between her eyebrows.

'Were you stroking some kind of animal?'

'It was nothing.'

'Don't lie,' she screams. 'You're hiding something from me. Something in this room.'

'No, honest.'

'Quiet,' she snaps. The mother gull is squawking out on the landing and a frightened peep is coming from under the bed. Mum lets go of my face.

'There's nothing here,' I say, trying to sound as normal

as I can. 'Let's go home.' Mum pulls a twig from the nest and blindly thrashes about under the bed.

'Don't.' I grab her wrist and yank the twig out of her hand. 'There's a little gull under there.'

'A little gull?' Mum's voice sounds unexpectedly gentle. 'You're hiding a gull chick in here?' She bites her lower lip and her face crumples. She starts to cry. 'You'd rather stroke that bird than be with me?' Her forehead almost bumps against mine. 'You should be with me,' she lisps, and sniffs to stop her nose running. 'If I ever find out you've been over here again...' She puts her mouth to my ear and whispers. 'I'll burn this hovel to the ground.' Her tears on my face make it look like I'm crying, too. 'Do you understand me?'

I nod. The white of her eyes is shot through with red. One of her front teeth is chipped at the corner.

'This is where you should be.' She slams her fist hard against her chest. Before I can say another word she's left the room and stormed downstairs.

I reach the window too late to watch her walk away. Waves are crashing against the rocks, clawing their way as far onto the island as they can. Flecks of foam fly across the beach.

44

On my way home it suddenly occurs to me I might not have closed the bedroom door tight enough and that my gull chick could escape. I hesitate, but I can't risk going back. First I have to see Mum. I worm my way into our garden through the brambles and the dark pine trees.

She must have been working in the garden before she came looking for me; the rake, hoe, and shovel are leaning against the shed. She's started digging here and there in the vegetable garden, I can't tell what for. Dried-out sunflower stalks are lying on the grass, clumps of sand still attached.

All the curtains in the house have been pulled shut. The back door is locked. After tugging at the handle a couple of times, I go round to the front door. I'm too late, she's locked it, too. I try to peek in through chinks in the curtains, but all the rooms are dark. The only light is coming from the kitchen, but I'm too scared to knock on the window and ask her to let me in. I have to do my best. She wants me to do my best to get in. It's up to me to make her feel that I want to be with her.

I go back into the garden. The little window in the toilet isn't shut tight. I pick up a thin stick and force it into the crack between window and frame to ease it open; it works.

I get a screwdriver from the shed and screw off the window stay, then haul myself up and squeeze through the gap. Once I'm inside, I'm not sure what to do next. I flush the toilet to let her know I'm here, and then wait till everything's quiet before I go into the hall.

Muffled voices are coming from the kitchen. I cough and carefully open the door. Mum and Karl turn round to face me at the same time.

'What have we here?' says Karl.

'There you are,' says Mum breezily. I can hardly bring myself to look at her. I don't even want to look at Karl. I know he's come to grass on me, to tell Mum I spat at him, and that I've been in his house, and now there'll be no making things right with her. I stare at the ground, like a petrified kid waiting for a slap. I'm just far enough away to dodge the first blow. To hit me, they'd both have to take a step in my direction, and I could be halfway up the stairs by that time.

'He's here,' says Mum with a smile and lays her hand on Karl's shoulder. *He*. Dad's white shirt is looking grubbier than it was a few days ago. One of the buttons has popped off. Surely Mum can see the disgusting way it's pulled tight around his belly?

'I'm glad you're here,' says Mum.

'Me?' I ask, looking up at her.

'He's come to tell us something.'

'Ask,' corrects Karl.

'To ask us something.'

Silence hangs between us. Water drips from the tap into the sink. I bite off a tender piece of white skin next to my thumbnail.

'What?'

'What d'you mean, what?' asks Karl.

'What did you want to ask us?'

'Uh... Jeez.'

He scratches under his woolly hat. If it crept any further up his head it would fall off. 'I've been thinking... Seems to me we're getting on much better these days. And with the nights drawing in... and because... well, just because... you know. I'm sitting over there most evenings. On my own, usually. I mean... usually all the time.'

'"Usually all the time"?' Mum repeats with a laugh.

Karl chuckles. 'Well, yeah... that's about the size of it.'

I find the nerve to straighten up a bit and my shoulders ease back a little.

'And cos we had such a good laugh here the other day when you were cutting my hair, I thought...' Karl coughs. 'Maybe you'd like to come over and watch TV with me sometime?' By the end of the question, his voice has gone up a couple of notches.

'Watch TV?' Mum teases.

'Or something else. I've got a deck of cards. Or we could just talk.'

'Over at your house?'

Karl nods.

'When?'

'Any old time.' He purses his lips. 'It's all one to me. Tomorrow. Or Saturday. Sometime after that. Before is okay, too.'

'So you're not fussed as to when?'

'Nah, 'course not. One evening's as long as the next. For me, anyway.'

'Just me?'

His little eyes dart nervously in my direction and then back to Mum. 'Yes,' he says as he breathes in.

'Without him?'

Karl nods. 'We need to make a go of things around here together, don't you reckon?'

Mum seems to be giving it some thought.

'Don't we?'

'Let's make it tonight then,' Mum says. I wait for her to burst out laughing, but she doesn't.

'Tonight?'

'Yes.'

'Great,' he says. 'That's just great.'

'Mikael, show him out, will you?' The door's still open, so all I have to do is grab the handle. As Karl squeezes past Mum, I watch as she steps forward, stands on his toes, and twists her foot like she's crushing a cigarette. All the while she looks straight at Karl and gives him a knowing smile. 'See ya later,' she says. Karl looks bewildered but manages a growly laugh.

Mum returns to the washing up she must have started before he came over. 'Right then, see ya later,' Karl
echoes. Mum doesn't answer. As he passes me at the
door, he pauses for a second and spits air at me. He heads
outside, roaring with laughter.

Cautiously I take the tea towel from its hook on the
fridge, go over, and stand next to Mum. My sideways
glances don't pick up anything out of the ordinary in
her expression. 'I'm sorry,' I say, but I'm not sure she can
hear me. 'Don't burn the place down. I promise I won't go
there anymore.' Mum continues to stare into the dish-
water.

I dry the dishes just the way she likes them done:
glasses first, then plates. Pots and pans last. If I see any
soap bubbles clinging to glasses or cutlery, I dip them
back into the water. My hand lingers in case hers wants
to accidentally brush against it.

45

The earrings Dad gave her as a present are dangling from
her ears. She leaves the house without saying anything
to me. It's already dark.

I crouch among the wet, rotting leaves beneath his window. From here I have a good view of what's going on
inside, but my face is still hidden in the dark. Karl has
tidied up his living room and draped a tablecloth over
the coffee table. The three chairs have been cleared away
so there's only the small settee to sit on. He invites Mum
to sit and plops down next to her.

Karl grabs the remote and starts flicking through the channels, pausing occasionally and looking at Mum for approval. A short answer from her, and his fat fingers start hitting the buttons again. When the remote doesn't respond, he slaps it against his leg before pointing it at the TV again. He races through the channels at least another four times and then drops the remote in Mum's lap with a chuckle. He picks it up, lets it fall again, and his grin widens. Mum responds with a little smile. The remote stays where Karl has dropped it. There's a film on I haven't seen before, about a man and a woman in a mint-green convertible. They drive around with the top down, and she perches on the back of her seat and blows bubbles with her gum. They keep having to run away from the motel where they've spent the night. Every time they end up in bed, the screen glows red and the camera turns away.

Meanwhile Karl yawns and casually stretches his arm along the back of the settee, behind Mum. She doesn't do anything to stop him. I try not to notice his arm and focus on what's happening in the film.

My fingers feel their way along the boards under the window and find a patch that's rotting away. I pick at it till there's a hole big enough for me to slide in three fingers.

A bunch of adverts flash past. There are two beer glasses on the table. Karl picks them up one after the other and wipes the rims on his sleeve. He fills them with beer, hands one to Mum, and clinks his glass against hers. It's strange to see her sitting next to him, as if she could be anyone. Not my mother, but a woman. She seems much smaller than when she's around me.

She gives a start and turns to look at the cuckoo clock above the door. Karl starts to laugh too loud. He points at the clock and imitates the way she jumped. It's nine o'clock.

The film continues, and Karl reaches for another can of beer. Before Mum can nod he tops up her glass and snakes his arm behind her again. Karl leans back into the settee and leers at Mum out of the corner of his eye as she looks at the screen. A shiver runs through her body as he lets his hand slide onto her shoulder. Instead of pushing his fleshy paw away, she turns toward the window. Our eyes meet for a frozen moment before I duck away.

She hasn't seen me. She can't have seen me. I hold my breath, not daring to get back up. I start counting to a hundred, but by the time I reach thirty, curiosity gets the better of me.

Lucky for me she's turned away from the window and is talking to Karl. I can't make out what she's saying. Maybe she's telling him to keep his fat hands to himself. He scratches his head.

His left hand feels at her thigh like he's testing a hot bath. He sits up straight. Mum puts her hand on his thigh and his touch turns rougher as he runs his hand up and down her leg. The film plays on.

Karl's hand disappears up her jumper. Her skin is pale and I can see her belly button. His hand is a bump moving around under the wool as he feels greedily at her breasts. Instead of slapping till he pulls it back, Mum lets him grab at her, both hands at once. Excitement shudders in my knees. Karl starts to bite and gnaw at her neck with his stinking mouth. She doesn't even turn her head away, though whenever Dad did that, she'd complain it tickled. I don't want to watch but I can't stop myself. Mum just keeps sitting there as Karl tries to unbutton her jeans. She says something to him and he falls back onto the settee like an obedient dog, mouth hanging open. He licks his lips and pulls open the buttons on his shirt. His nipples are piggy pink. Flustered, he tugs down his trousers and his sausage dick springs into view, pale and crooked. Lying back, chin on chest, he gazes proudly at himself, my mum, and his stiff dick. Mum leans toward him and wraps her fist around it.

I feel sick. With Karl, myself, Mum. With the fact I'm seeing any of this. My own dick is getting harder in my pants and I can't make it stop. I scrabble among the wet leaves that surround me and grab the first big stone I can find. I take a few steps back and hurl it as hard as I can through the window.

Glass comes clattering down in huge, jagged pieces. The stone thuds onto the table and shatters a vase. Mum shrinks back, hands shielding her face. Karl tries to jump up and their weight tips the settee over backward. The little lace curtain in the top window crashes to the floor, rail and all.

Everything goes quiet for a second or two, apart from the chatter of the TV. Swaying shards of glass hang in the window frame like pointed guillotines. One of them smashes down onto the windowsill.

'The little fucker!' comes a voice from inside. 'The stupid little fucker!' Karl has leapt to his feet but doesn't come any closer to the window. Maybe he's scared I'll throw something else. 'Look what he's done.' He picks up the stone and shows it to Mum. 'Go on, look!' he screams. He stamps through the room, holding up his trousers with one hand. 'That boy of yours is a nut job. A fucking lunatic. My whole window smashed to bits.' I back away till I'm standing in the dark. 'Out there spying on us. Jesus! And then he wrecks the whole fucking place.'

Mum straightens her bra under her jumper, buttons

up her jeans, and takes her raincoat from the chair. 'Don't go, please. Stay,' Karl begs. 'We can go upstairs. There's a bed. And a heater.' Like fighting two fires at once, he switches between cursing me and the broken window and pleading with Mum to stay. The wind shreds and scatters his curses. I run for home.

Not long after I've closed the bedroom door behind me, I hear Mum come in. I turn the key in the lock and sit on my bed with the blanket pulled over me. I get up again, unlock the door, and then wonder whether I should lock it again. I end up leaving it open.

Mum climbs the stairs. I hear her pause outside my door, but she goes on up to her room. Over at Karl's house, light is shining from every window.

I lie down on the bed and turn off the light. With my eyes closed, even the slightest sound makes me jump. I picture Karl creeping into my room and towering above my bed. I scare myself so much I can barely make myself open my eyes to see if he's really there.

That night I dream my little gull chick has taken shelter under my bed. Karl pulls the bed aside with one hand and grabs the chick in the other. Little Gull screams in terror. Karl slices him open on the kitchen table, claws out the organs with his fingers, and stuffs them in his mouth. Little Gull is peeping and crying all the while. 'Got to do it while they're alive,' Karl says over and over, his mouth full. 'Got to do it while they're alive.' He pulls tufts of hair from his head and starts stuffing the wailing chick. He forces wire through the legs and makes the chick stand still as its cries grow louder and louder. He sews up the wound with fishing line and nails my little gull to a piece of wood. 'Look,' says Karl. 'Still alive.'

I jump up and reach in panic for the lamp beside my

bed, but it's not there. That was my old room. I tug on the cord above the bed. The ceiling light flickers on and I squint into the glare.

There's no one else in the room. My sheets are damp with sweat. I sit up and look over at Karl's house. Moonlight reflects in the dark of his bedroom window and a tarpaulin is flapping at the window downstairs.

A shiver runs through my chest. I lie back down and leave the light on.

46

I have to do this.

I take the top one from each pile. I close my eyes and my arms feel their way inside the jumper. My head finds the hole in the neck. The jeans are much too big, but I pull them tight around my hips with his belt. Even the socks I put on are his. I can't bring myself to look in the mirror, and head straight downstairs.

Mum is hunched over her bowl of porridge. I've promised myself I'll stand in the doorway as long as it takes for her to look at me. The label on the jumper itches my neck. I resist the urge to scratch and keep my arms stiff at my sides. I have to do this.

Minutes tick by before Mum notices me. A smile appears on her face. Her eyes narrow as she looks at me and begins to nod. 'Lovely,' she says. 'They look good on you, really good.' She runs her fingers along the waistband of the jeans and feels how the jumper hangs off my shoulders. 'The rest will take care of itself.'

'What do you mean?'

'Oh, I'll help you with that, love.' She brings a hesitant hand to my face. I pull back a little. 'Don't be afraid. No need for that, is there?'

'I'm not afraid.'

'Good.'

I want to say something about last night, but I don't know how to start without breaking something in her smile. I keep seeing flashes of her white skin, Karl's groping hands, his face getting redder and redder. His stiff dick poking out of his jeans. And Mum's hands. To me they were always just her hands. I never thought they could wrap around a man's dick so easily. Those same hands are holding the handle of the frying pan and taking the salt cellar from the spice rack. Only now there's something strange and secretive about them.

'Could you turn the radio on?'

'Okay.'

Dad's jeans might get dirty if I climb up on the draining board, so I pull over a chair to stand on.

'That sounds good,' says Mum when I turn the dial. 'Leave it there.'

'What are you cooking?'

'Something for you.'

Without asking, she's making me an omelette and frying up half a pack of bacon.

'That's a lot of bacon.'

'I thought you liked bacon.'

'I do,' I say. 'But there won't be enough for you.'

'I don't want any.'

Rasher after rasher sizzles in the hot pan, sending up a greyish haze. 'This should fill you out a bit.' She squeezes my upper arm. 'Around here.'

The sun colours the kitchen orange. It's hanging low and won't rise much higher today. Mum flops my omelette onto a plate, puts it on the table, and sits down opposite to watch me eat.

'Tasty?'

'Mmm.'

Her chin resting on her hand, Mum looks at me intently. Even my most unthinking movements feel awkward. The neck of the jumper is still too wide, but seems to be tightening around my throat. It's as if Dad's clothes are coming back to life with me inside them, changing shape with every move as he closes in around me. Yet Mum's stare makes me feel like I've raided the dressing-up box. I get up to fetch a glass.

'More salt on your omelette?'

'No. Just getting some water.'

'Is it too salty?'

'It's just right.'

'Here, drink mine.' She hands me her half-full glass. 'One less to wash up.'

I sink back into my chair. The water is clear but somehow it turns my stomach, as if Mum's already had it in her mouth. The rim bears the imprint of her lips.

'Something wrong?'

I shake my head.

'Drink up, then.'

With the imprint of her mouth on the other side, I put the glass to my lips and gulp the water down so I don't have to taste it. I walk over to the tap, fill the glass again, and drain it in one go.

'My. You *are* thirsty.'

I wipe my mouth with the back of my hand.

'Sure your omelette's not too salty?'

'My omelette is fine.'

There's a hammering at the door. My whole body pounds to the thud of my heartbeat. 'Who's there?' asks Mum, as if it could be anyone but Karl.

'Me,' he says.

'It's not locked!' shouts Mum.

Karl marches in. 'About last night.' He scratches under his woolly hat. 'How are we going to sort this out?'

'Sort what out?'

'Thanks to your loony son, I'm freezing my arse off over there.'

'My loony son?'

'Chucking a stone through my window while we're having a good time together. Don't act like you don't know what I'm on about.'

'And you are...?'

'What d'you mean, *you are?*'

'Has this gentleman introduced himself?' Mum asks me. Thoughts snail through my head. I don't know what to say. 'I didn't catch his name. Did you?'

'It's Karl,' I say.

'Playing silly buggers now, are we?'

'Fat,' she says.

'Bloody right. A big fat bill.'

'Fatso.'

'What did you call me?'

'Fat. Fatty. Fatso.'

'Look, I don't know what your little game is, but...'

'A big fat man with a crooked white dick.'

'Aha!' Karl grins proudly. 'Got yer memory back, at least.'

'Next time keep your filthy paws off me.'

'Don't you worry,' Karl barks. 'I've no stomach for that scraggy old meat of yours.'

Mum keeps her arms crossed high against her chest. I

copy her so it looks more like we belong together. 'Yeah, keep your fat paws off her,' I say, surprised at how fierce I sound. 'She's not yours.'

'Go fuck yerself.' Karl prods my arm. 'I used to think you were just a sad little bugger with a dead dad. Looks like nothing's changed.'

'You're not allowed to say that,' I bite back.

'I'll say whatever the fuck I want. So you can bugger off and keep out of my way from now on.'

'Bet you thought you could fuck me,' sneers Mum. 'But I'm not a filthy whore like your Pernille.'

There's a silence. Karl clenches his jaw. 'I don't care who coughs up for that window, you or that son of yours. But it's going to be paid for.'

Mum thrusts a finger to within an inch of his nose. 'Call him "that son of mine" one more time...'

'Hah! Threats now, is it?'

Mum's hand claws at my shoulder and pulls me between them. 'It would seem this fat gentleman doesn't know your name. Introduce yourself.'

Karl keeps his hands at his sides.

'Go on, shake Fatso's hand and introduce yourself,' hisses Mum. I hold out a timid hand in his direction.

Karl's Adam's apple bobs up and down. 'Crazy bitch. Off yer heads, the pair of you.' He charges out of the kitchen, slamming the door so hard the contents of the cupboards clink and tremble.

'Fat-so, Fat-so, Fat-so,' Mum croons to the sing-song rhythm of an abandoned swing. I want to go upstairs and take off Dad's clothes, but I don't dare leave the kitchen. In my head all I can hear is, 'Dad's dead, Dad's dead, Dad's dead.'

47

Early in the evening, she heats some tinned meat in a saucepan and mashes it up with yesterday's spaghetti. 'Set the table, will you?' Extra sauce is bubbling in another pan. I lay two plates across from each other, knife and fork on either side.

'Could you get out the thick table mats, too?' We never use them, but I know they're kept in the bottom drawer. Mum puts the pans on the mats and stirs the contents with a wooden spoon.

'Good,' she says. 'Extra large portion for you today.' It turns out to be a daunting mound of food, almost double the amount on her plate. The spaghetti is carpeted in lumpy tomato sauce. The carrots she's mixed in are the size of little fingertips, and so soft I can squish them against the roof of my mouth with my tongue. I eat as much as I can, without complaining. Every time I think I've had enough, I scrape what's left to one side and casually lay my knife and fork on top.

'Aren't you going to eat that?' She points her knife at the strings of pasta and the pinkish meat on my plate.

'Forgot,' I murmur.

Done at last, I slide my plate toward the middle of the table.

'What an appetite,' she smiles. 'Finished the lot.'

'Tasty,' I say.

'Yeah? In that case, I'm sure you can polish this off, too.' She picks up her plate, tilts it over mine, and scrapes her leftovers onto it.

'It was really nice Mum, but...' I puff out my cheeks and rub my belly. She stares at me till I pick up my knife and fork and clear my plate.

48

It's morning when I wake to find Mum in bed beside me again. Something tickles my face and I half-dream it's a moth fluttering past my cheek. I open my eyes. Mum is looking straight at me. 'What's the matter?' I say, and take a startled look around the room. She's lying close to me under the covers.

'No need to jump,' she whispers. 'It's only me.'

'Have you been lying here all this time?'

'All what time?'

'All night. I didn't notice.'

'You were sound asleep. That's good. You must have needed it.' Her hand appears from under the blanket and an outstretched finger moves toward my face.

'Come a little closer.' Her finger strokes my upper lip, so softly I can hardly feel it. Dimples appear at the corners of her mouth. 'Don't forget to shave, cactus face.'

I rub a few grains of sleep from the corner of my eye.

'Did I wake you up?'

'Maybe.'

'You go back to sleep now.' She turns and sits up on the edge of the bed. She stretches her arms, cracks her knuckles, and ties back her hair without looking. As she heads for the shower, she smooths down her wide night-shirt and tugs at one side of her knickers where they've ridden up between her buttocks.

49

The cupboard under the stairs is empty. 'Do you know where the grocery crates are?'

'Take a look at the quay.'

I half-open the curtains. 'Have you put them out already?'

'Uh-huh.'

'But that's my job.' The door is locked and the key's not in it. 'D'you know where the front-door key is?'

'Yes,' she says chirpily. 'But the crates are ready and waiting.'

I walk over to her. 'I know, but I still have to give Ingmar our list for next time.'

'Already taken care of.' She puts her hand on my shoulder. 'Just wait here till the grocery boy has left his crates. Or are you dying to tell him something you can't tell me?' Her eyebrows arch into a question.

'Good,' says Mum. 'The quicker he's done, the quicker you can bring them in.'

The dog pokes its head above the bow and disappears again. It pops up again further along, paws and all this time, pointed ears sticking straight up. I sit on my bedroom windowsill, cheek resting against the cold glass, and watch through my binoculars. Ingmar casts a line smoothly around a post on the quay and moors his boat. His dog sits down on the deck in front of him and lets a green tennis ball drop from its mouth. Ingmar picks up the ball, extends his arm, and pretends to throw. The dog leaps excitedly onto the quay and bounds after the ball that isn't there. Once it notices, it slows down and turns around. Ingmar stretches his arm again, reaches back, and this time the ball bounces onto the island and disappears among the brambles. Ears flattened against its head and tail straight as a stick, the dog tears after the ball. The green tarpaulin is still flapping around in front of Karl's broken window.

Another figure emerges from the cabin of the grocery boat, in a long padded coat that makes her look like a shapeless snowman. Brown hair whips the furry trim of her hood. Ingmar pinches her backside as he walks past. It must be Mikaella. She gets in Ingmar's way as he lugs our full crates onto the quay.

Ingmar puts his fingers to his mouth and whistles. His dog comes slinking out of the bramble bushes, belly hugging the ground but no tennis ball in its mouth. It races toward the boat and lands on the deck with a single jump. Ingmar scratches between its ears. The dog dances around the hooded girl and sits panting in front of her, tongue lolling out of its mouth. Ingmar grabs it roughly by the collar and drags it into the cabin. A V of geese passes overhead. The chug of the boat's engine grows louder again.

Ingmar hasn't looked at our house once.

'The groceries are here!' Mum shouts up to me. 'Could you fetch them in?'

I go downstairs. 'Give me the key then.'

'Door's already open.'

I can still hear the chugging of the boat when I get to the crates. It's coming from just around the bend by the rocks. With my back to the house I zip open the leather postal pouch and flick through the bank statements and Mum's magazines. Nothing special.

The chugging stops.

I listen, but all I can hear is wind, gulls, and sea.

Keeping an eye out in case Mum follows me, I climb over the rocks and out to the point of the bay. The boat is rocking like a cradle on the waves, thirty feet away at most. The hooded girl is leaning against the rail of the bow, looking bored. The hatch on the deck is open.

'Have you broken down?'

The girl jumps and glares at me. 'How long have you been standing there?'

'I heard the engine conk out. Is something broken?'

'It's probably nothing. My boyfriend thinks he's a proper sailor, but sometimes he just twiddles the knobs.' She zips open her coat and takes out a pack of chewing gum, pulls off the wrapper, and lets it blow away on the wind. I can see the shape of her breasts under her coat, but I'm afraid she'll notice if I take a good look.

'You must be Mikaella.'

'How do you know?'

'Ingmar told me.'

'Who are you, then?'

'We have the same name. Nearly.'

'How come?'

'I'm Mikael.'

'Oh.'

'Try to start her up again,' says a voice from down in the hold.

'I'm talking.'

'Who to?'

'That boy.'

Ingmar climbs up on deck and shakes the grimy gloves from his hands. I want to say hello, but he grins and puts a finger to his lips. I signal back with my eyebrows. 'Do you live in Tramsud, too?' I ask, to keep Mikaella talking. She answers but I only half hear cos I'm watching Ingmar sneak up behind her. His hands shoot around and grab her breasts.

'No groping!' Mikaella snarls at him over her shoulder. 'You know I don't like it.'

'Tripped and needed something to hold onto,' Ingmar

chuckles. 'Sorry.' Their voices carry across the water. It's as if I'm standing right next to them.

'One little kiss,' he pleads. 'And I'll never grope 'em again.'

'Never?'

He nods his head obediently. Mikaella takes her chewing gum out of her mouth and presses her lips to his. I'm not sure, but I think I see a flash of tongue. They both have their eyes closed.

Ingmar has me to thank for that kiss. Well, a bit, anyway.

'Okay then,' says Ingmar. 'Let's see if I can't get this heap of junk back up and running.' He ducks into the cabin. The engine coughs, splutters, and begins to rev. Shame. Mikaella shoots me a sidelong glance from under her hood. Ingmar taps his forehead with two fingers.

'Cheerio!' I shout.

50

A few days later, Mum is lying on the settee with her head on a pile of cushions. Growly snores are coming from her throat and her mouth is hanging open, limp and hollow. I feel the bedroom key in my trouser pocket. I've locked the door from outside, so if she wakes up suddenly and comes looking for me, she'll think I've locked myself in my room. It might make her angry again, but not as angry as knowing where I'm going.

My raincoat is hanging over the back of Dad's chair, right where she can see it. I plonk my boots in the middle of the doormat. When I get back I'll have to sneak up to my room as quietly as possible, unlock the door, and then stamp back down the stairs.

In my socks I run over the path that winds round the island to the right. It's not the shortest route, but it means I can't be seen from Karl's house. Along the way I pick up all the mussels, cockles, and other shells I can find. I even come across a small crab and graze my wrist trying to pick it up. A couple of times my feet almost slip out from under me on the smooth stones. My toes are numb with cold, but the faster I run, the less I notice.

'It was all I could find,' I say, dumping the crab and the shells on the bed. 'It'll have to do for now.' Gull is in a state after me charging in like that. She flaps around the room in a panic and the rush of air from her wings sends dust and feathers flying. The whole place is white with bird shit. Little Gull cries along with her. When I try to calm him down, he hides under the bed. 'I'm not allowed to come here anymore, but I'm going to come and get you. Then we'll set your mother free and I'll take you with me. As soon as I've found a good place for you. I'll think of something. I promise.'

Gull has pounced on the food I've brought and snaps at the crab. She stands on it and rips the legs from its body with her beak. The crab tries desperately to sink its claws into some part of her, but it's grabbing at thin air. I crush a few shells under my heel and toss them under the bed. 'That's for you, Little Gull.'

In my rush to get upstairs I didn't notice, but as I'm leaving, I see the bead curtain has been torn down and is lying on the floor. I step over it and go into the kitchen.

Our three chairs are standing around an empty space. Four table legs are lying in the corner next to the stove, splintered fragments of tabletop still attached. Mum! It's a trap, a test. If I say anything about this, she'll know I've been here. I pick up one of the table legs. It's heavy as a club, and I feel a tremendous urge to smash something. I just don't know what. My heart is pounding in my throat. The black paint on the floor where Miss Augusta's chair stood is worn away to the bare wood. Where our chairs once stood, the boards are as black as the rest of the floor. There's not a trace of where we used to sit. I put the chairs back in place around the table that's no longer there.

51

'Where have you been?'

'Nowhere.'

'You shouldn't go out without your coat.' She continues to stare at the teabag she's dunking in the pot. 'And definitely not in your socks.'

'I had to run over to the shed.'

'Just like that?'

'To get a hammer.'

'So where is it?'

'I've just put it back. I was finished with it.'

'I didn't hear any hammering.'

'That's cos you were asleep.'

'Mikael?' She looks up at me through a veil of hair. 'You know what I said about Pernille's place.'

'I don't go there anymore. Honest.' She lets the teabag drip over the sink, then flips open the lid of the pedal bin. Scraps of sentences tumble through my head, things I want to say, to needle her, to show her I know about the smashed-up table, but without giving myself away. Words that will make her feel sorry for what she's done.

'We're going to tidy up.'

'Tidy what up?'

'This, for example.' She grabs my raincoat by the hood and pulls it off the back of Dad's chair. 'This belongs on the coat rack.'

'And what else?'

'Junk.'

'What kind of junk?'

'Things that are getting in our way.'

'Is our table in the way, too?' I ask, trying to sound as offhand as possible.

'No,' she laughs. 'It's fine where it is.' She opens a kitchen cupboard at random and puts her hands on her hips. 'This, for example.' From the bottom of a pile of dishes, she pulls out my baby plate. The three bears on it have almost been scratched off by all the times she and Dad cut my meals up into bite-sized chunks.

'That's my plate from when I was little.'

'Exactly. Hasn't been used in ages.' She runs her fingertips over what's left of the bears, then lets the plate fall to pieces on the floor. I try to catch it, but I haven't a hope. 'We've got stacks of other plates,' she says soothingly.

It's shattered into too many pieces to ever be glued back together.

'And this is just gathering dust.' It's the little boat on top of the cupboard, the one I made years ago from bits of driftwood and shells. On tiptoe she can just reach it.

'That's the boat I made for your birthday.'

'And now I don't want it anymore.' The little mast breaks easily. To crack open the bow, she has to press hard with her thumbs.

'You don't have to smash it up. I'll throw it away.'

'Fine,' she says, and hands me the wreckage.

My fishing rod is leaning against the wall behind the banister, untouched since Dad disappeared. 'This can go, too,' she says.

'Give it to me. I'll take it out to the shed.'

Mum puts her foot on the second stair and lays the rod across her knee. The wood bends a little before it breaks.

'Why are you doing this?' I ask.

'Don't start making a fuss.' She hands me both halves of the fishing rod, still threaded together with fishing line. I follow her upstairs with the boat and the broken rod.

'Couldn't we have put all this stuff in the shed? Or up in the attic?'

'Hoarding isn't the same as clearing up.' She stands at the top of the stairs and takes a look around. 'Can't see anything here that needs throwing away.'

In my room she opens the doors to her old wardrobe, where my clothes are neatly piled.

'What should we do with this lot?'

'How d'you mean?'

'You know fine and well what I mean.'

'Those are my clothes.'

'I'm a woman. And a woman needs her own space.'

'But you've got a wardrobe upstairs.'

'And where do I sleep?'

'Up in the attic.'

She nods toward the bed with a knowing look.

I swallow. 'Here sometimes, too.'

'Well then,' she says. One sweep of her arm, and my T-shirts are lying on the floor.

'D'you want us to change rooms again?'

'I want you to clear all this up.'

'Why should I?'

'Trust a man to say that,' she sighs. Before I can catch my breath, she's out of the room. I run after her again. 'Stop traipsing around behind me. Clear up first. I'll make a start upstairs.'

Glancing outside, I notice that Karl has boarded up his broken window. I get my binoculars. It's Miss Augusta's tabletop. He's nailed it in place, coffee rings facing outward, turned it into just another lump of wood. Fat sausage-dick bastard! Mum didn't smash the table, it was fucking Fatso over there.

'Close your eyes.' I hear her voice behind me and automatically turn to face the door. 'Stop! Close your eyes first.' I cover them with my hands.

'No peeking?' I hear her coming closer, then feel her waving something in front of my face.

'Can't see a thing. Honest.'

'Okay. Now you can look.' She's holding one leg awkwardly in the air, a pointed foot inches from my nose. Three of her toenails are varnished.

'Red,' I say.

'Pretty?'

'Yes, I think so.'

'Then I'll do the rest, too. Or should I pick another colour?'

'Red is fine.'

'Your favourite colour,' she says.

52

I'm lying awake. The things in my room are starting to emerge from the dark: the wardrobes, my desk, the chair at the foot of the bed. First they get their shape back. Then they're steeped in the dark blue of early morning. That's my real favourite colour.

The door squeaks softly. Mum must have tiptoed down from the attic. I lie on my back, pull the covers up under my chin, and pretend to be asleep. Through half-closed eyes I watch her creep into the room. Naked, apart from her knickers. Cold air rushes in as she lifts the bed-clothes. She lies down on her side, facing me, and curls up so close I feel dizzy.

A hair tickles my ear when she moves. I don't dare scratch it. My whole body strains to resist the itch. Between the sheets I can feel the nearness of her warm skin, her breath. If I turn to face her, my nose will brush against hers. Her breasts are right next to my arm. I lie there, tense, eyes shut tight. The slightest twitch of my toes feels like a landslide. I wait. Outside, the sun has come up.

I feel smothered by her nearness, but as soon as she turns away to the other side of the bed, I miss her warmth. I hold my breath, wait for a moment or two, then turn toward her. I could lay my hand against her back and scratch gently between her shoulder blades, like she'd ask me to when she had an itch she couldn't reach. I would keep on scratching till she moaned softly.

She rolls back suddenly. Startled, I roll with her and we both lie there on our backs.

My hand tingles with a kind of hunger for skin. I run my hand over the mattress as lightly as I can. A rough edge of fingernail catches on a loop in the towelling sheet. My hand seems to have a heart of its own, pumping blood and heat to my fingertips. I can't stop it from edging toward her, one millimetre at a time. Much sooner than I expect, my hand finds hers. 'Sorry,' I whisper. She doesn't reply, but I can see from the glimmer of her eyes that she's awake. We're lying so close together that it could still have been an accident.

A shiver runs through me as her little finger touches mine. Her hand climbs tentatively onto my hand, like a crab onto a stone. Her palm feels moist, I hear her swallow. One of her fingers begins to rub slowly back and forth across my knuckles. My hand no longer feels like it's part of me.

In an almost involuntary motion, our hands glide upward. She doesn't take hold of my hand, nor do I lift hers. It happens all by itself, like metal and magnet attracting. With her free hand she pushes the blanket down below her hips, exposing her naked breasts, close to my face. The left one is hanging a little to the side.

Slowly her hand guides me along her thigh, so very close but not quite touching, over the black knickers that score her skin where the washed-out lace around the elastic has frayed. It's as if she's directing my hand toward a lump beneath her skin and wants me to feel it, too, cos she doesn't know what it is and it wasn't there yesterday. Our hands move up over her stomach, rising and falling with her breath. The turning of our elbows becomes a firm but gentle hold that forces me onto my side. Her mouth is half open, her eyes are closed. I follow our slow hands as they hover over her body as if, inch by inch, she is trying to sense whether this is where they should land. They come closer to the dull, smooth skin of her breasts. She glides my hand over them at a hair's breadth. A greenish-blue vein meanders beneath the skin, the brown rings of her nipple contract.

With a sudden squeeze, she presses my hand to her breast. Her stomach jerks and tenses and her knees force the blanket up. Her mouth opens wide and gasps for breath. My blood seems to shiver, like a chill has crept under my skin. My tongue is thick; it tingles. A deep sigh escapes from her mouth and her breasts sink. Her nipple softens slightly beneath my palm.

My arm turns heavy as a dead fish. I take hold of my elbow and carefully pull my hand out from under hers. I move my fingers till numbness turns to prickling, then tingling. Mum turns toward me and her warm breath tickles my neck. I feel the shock of her hand against my stomach. The muscles tense and she follows the contraction, stroking down past my belly button. 'Birk,' she whispers. 'My own sweet Birk.'

Everything around me tilts and lurches. The urge to run is all I can feel. I try to get up and almost crash to the floor, fighting for air, as if I've fallen through the ice and I'm struggling desperately to find the hole I fell through.

'Why don't you come back here and lie down?' Mum asks, raising her head and propping herself up on her elbows. 'It's early yet.'

I stumble out of the room, grab the banister, and pull myself up the stairs to the attic. I have to make a conscious effort to lift my feet from one step to the next. I hear her voice behind me. 'What are you going up there for?' The door to my old room is open. Teeth chattering, I crawl inside, shut the door behind me with trembling hands, and turn the key twice in the lock. Mum comes up the stairs. Her words reach me through the door. 'You're back now. You can't leave me again.' Her knocking turns to dull thudding, and soon her fists are battering against the door. It strains at the hinges. 'What are you doing in there? You should be with me.'

The wind howls in when I open the window. It's cold, full of winter. Jagged strips of wallpaper have been torn from the wall where pencil lines used to mark how much I'd grown. Same goes for the drawings I did on the wall above where my desk once stood. Mum's clothes are scattered all around the room, the fallout from a dozen failed attempts to sort, fold, and stack them. The slats from my bed have been trampled to pieces and the mattress is lying on the floor. It feels like an embrace when I lie down on it. Clouds rise from my mouth with every breath. Mum's voice murmurs and pleads at the other side of the door. I pull the blanket over me, but the smell of her is too strong. I fling it off and wrap myself in a curtain that's lying in a heap on the floor. Knees pulled tight to my chest, I fall asleep.

53

It's almost afternoon by the time I wake up. The room is hazy with smoke. A thick black cloud is blowing around the house, coming from the back garden. I can't see the fire from my attic room, but I can hear it pop and crackle. Mum must have decided to burn some rubbish.

I slink down the stairs, one step at a time. Birk, she called me. Birk. Birk. I can still feel the warmth of her breast beneath my hand.

To avoid bumping into Mum, I walk along the front of the house and step into the garden from there. Pointed tongues of flame lick at overhanging branches that dance and sway in the heat. Some have turned black. The fire is much too close to the house and the walls are flickering bright orange. Over by the shed I see the empty fuel tank from the lawnmower. The cap is missing.

Her face turned away from the heat, Mum appears in the doorway, clutching armfuls of stuff. She throws everything she's holding onto the burning pile. Then she flings a pair of shoes into the flames. My shoes. Orange sparks fly up. 'What are you doing? They're not even old,' I shout. She doesn't hear me.

Next, she takes one of my jumpers and dangles it by the sleeve, making sure it catches fire before she lets it fall. Thick, fuzzy smoke rises as the wool turns black. She tosses a full bag onto the fire. The plastic melts and the clothes she's stuffed into it burst out. 'Stop!' I scream. 'Those things are mine!' Mum has gone back into the house.

I want to get closer, try to salvage something, but the heat is much too strong. I run around the blaze. It's only then that I see the charred carcass of my desk, the cuddly toys that lived at the foot of my bed for years, the red football Karl gave me, soft around the edges. Even my chair at the kitchen table is there among the flames, glowing fibres from the basket seat whirling through the air. A little mound of dripping, bubbling plastic... my binoculars! It's so much, I feel deadened.

Everything turns black in the snarling blaze. An upstairs window swings open. 'What are you doing?' I scream up at her. 'All this stuff is mine. Keep your hands off it.' I see in her face that she can hear me. She holds out the jar of feathers I saved, turns it upside down, and shakes till it's empty. The heat blasts the feathers skyward but the flames leap up and swallow them. Spinning and burning, they fall to the ground. She throws the jar down into the yard and it shatters on the paving stones. 'No! Don't! You have to stop,' I plead. 'Stop, please.' I go to run inside.

'Stay right where you are!' she yells. 'If you come up here, I'll jump.' I stay rooted to the spot. Mum takes a step back as if she's getting ready to lunge forward.

'No! Don't jump! I'll stay here. Only stop. Please stop.'

Coughing, she reappears at the open window and starts throwing books onto the fire like blocks of wood. First the volumes of my encyclopaedia, then my comics. Last of all she picks up my atlas and starts ripping out the pages.

'Don't, please. Stop, stop, stop.' Orphaned continents flutter down. I want to grab them in mid-air, run into the fire to catch them, but the heat forces me back. Africa, the North Pole, the maps of the ocean currents that never brought Dad back. All I can do is stare.

A scrap of paper lands at my feet. It's the swimming certificate Dad made for me: *testimony that Mikael Hammermann can.* The rest is charred. I pick it up and put it in my pocket.

Mum has come down into the garden. Her hands slide under my arms and she tries to hug me from behind. Her fingers lock together and she pulls me tighter toward her. Everything she says sounds like it's coming from far away. She circles me and puts her hands to my face. 'I've been very thorough. You'll be so proud of me.'

'Now I've lost everything,' I whisper.

She plants soothing kisses on my neck, my cheeks. Presses her lips to my forehead. My chest judders and snot drips from my chin. 'I have nothing left. Nothing at all.' The words lurch from my mouth.

'They're only things, love. Things that were getting in our way. I've got rid of them. For us.' Her eyes have turned watery and red. 'You're making me cry but I'm not sad. It's for the best, you'll see.' She sniffs. I turn away but she tugs so hard at my neck that her mouth is right next to my ear. 'You have me to love.'

As if she's going to propose, she goes down on her knees. 'One last thing. I forgot,' she says sweetly, pressing a fist tenderly against the back of my knee. 'Just let me have your boots. Please. Then all you'll have left to get used to is your name.' She looks up at me. 'My very own Birk.'

My knee slams into her shoulder, a jolt so sudden it's like I didn't even want it to happen. The toe of my boot strikes her full in the stomach. Without a sound, Mum falls over backward. She looks up at me like a startled deer. 'You kicked me,' she whimpers, and looks at her stomach as if her pain is written there. 'You kicked me here.' She curls up and begins to sob. Shocked by what I've done, I want to comfort her, to help her up, but I can't. Mum lies there on the grass like a toppled chair. I run from her.

She'll burn everything. Everything that belongs to me. I have to free my gull chick before she sets fire to Miss Augusta's house. Little Gull can't stay there. He has to fly.

When I get there I'll chase his mother out of the bedroom and take Little Gull gently in my hands. It won't matter anymore if he smells of me, cos soon he won't need anyone but himself.

I'll have to be careful with him. If I'm not scared, he won't be either. I need to hold him without hurting him, but tight enough to calm him down. I'll stroke his neck with my finger and whisper to him that he's a sky sailor. He doesn't know it yet, but he can fly. No one has to teach him how, it's always been inside him. I'll open the window and give him to the wind.

My hands are shaking so much, it takes me a while to get the bedroom door open. Gull shoots past my legs and hurtles down the stairs, flapping and stumbling. The room is quiet. It takes me a moment or two to notice.

'Little Gull?'

He's not in the nest or behind the curtains. I even take a look out on the landing, just to be sure.

I get down on the floor and lie flat on my stomach so I can look under the bed. There's something lying there. I stretch out my arm but I can't reach. I pull the bed aside.

It's Little Gull. Legs folded. Bones as thin as twigs, barely held together by a film of skin. Both his eyes are missing, his skull is an empty walnut shell. His body creaks as I pick him up by the tips of his wings and spread them. Empty. A hollow cage of ribs. It's as if he's shrunk away to nothing so he can fit back into his egg.

It's my fault. His mother has pecked him to death, and it's my fault. I should never have locked them up. I should have fed them more often. Maybe his mother waited as long as she could, pecking at empty shells, trying to eat feathers plucked from the ripped pillow, hacking away at the rotten wood of the windowsill. Her chick kept tapping his little beak against hers, begging with his mouth open wide, peeping higher and higher. He couldn't last a day without her, but all she had was hunger. A hunger growing too strong to deny.

Little Gull opened his beak patiently, expecting to be fed at last.

But she pecked him to death.

Desperately, I scrabble around for feathers, down, and shreds of skin, gathering them together as if Little Gull was made of pieces I can fit back together. As if I can return him to his nest and get his mother to hatch him all over again. Tears blur everything around me. I press Little Gull to my chest with one hand and crawl across the room. I want to disappear behind the curtains or under the bed.

I open the wardrobe with my free hand and disappear among the coats and skirts. I shut the door behind me. In the darkness, all that's left is the panting of my breath and the little bird in my hands. One of the hangers comes crashing down, and I pull the fallen coat over me like a blanket.

I will stay here forever.

54

One winter it was so cold that even the sea froze over. Not all the way out, just along the shore. Dad took me outdoors with him. Our boots made creaky footprints in the snow. The water had hardened into sheets and peaks that ground against one another like there wasn't enough room, even though they had a whole sea behind them.

'Mum told me that's not allowed,' I said as Dad climbed onto one of the ice sheets. He stepped from one to the next, balancing with outstretched arms. 'Can *you* see Mum?'

I looked around. Everything was white.

'If you can't see Mum, she can't see us, either.' He held out his hands to me. 'Come on.'

'The two of us might fall through.'

'No, we won't.'

'Are you sure?'

'Stay close enough to me and the ice will think we're one person. And then it won't let us fall through.' It was slippery under my soles, and the ice was sharp at the edges. We clambered out over another few ice sheets. Standing on a flat section, Dad carefully lifted me up and held me close. 'Now the ice thinks we're one person.'

Snowflakes drifted down. It was weird how they didn't lie on the surface of the deep-blue waves. 'The South Pole is that-a-way,' said Dad with his cheek against mine. It was a little bit scratchy.

'I'm going to live with you my whole life.'

He smiled. 'That's what you think now.'

'That's what I'll always think.'

'There will come a day when you'll want to leave. This island will get too small for you.'

'Nah, it'll always be the same size.'

'But you won't be.'

'Well, then I'll start my own island. Over there.' I pointed my mitten at the spot where the ice met the slurping waves. 'If I throw a rock in the same place every day, eventually an island will appear.'

Dad grinned.

'And then I'll be your neighbour.'

'I'd like that,' he said.

'But for now, we're still one person.'

Snowflakes settled on his eyebrows.

55

I see something glinting in the dark among the coats
and skirts in the wardrobe. Two eyes. 'Dad?'

I hear him moving toward me. His rough hands reach
out for mine. One by one he peels open my clenched fingers to feel what I'm holding.

'What is it?' he whispers.

'It's my little gull.'

'He's dead.'

'It's my fault. I should have set him free.'

'Did you try to love him?'

'I think so.'

'Then you're not to blame. Bury him somewhere.'

'Can you keep him for me?'

'You'll have to do that yourself. You're the one who
loves him.'

'Dad?'

A pack of cigarettes rustles. The flame from the lighter
illuminates his face.

'You traded your life for mine.'

'What do you mean?'

'When you saved me, did you swap us around?'

The tip of the cigarette glows in the dark.

'Who are you?'

'I'm Mikael.'

'Dad?'

'Yes.'

'I miss you.'

On the Design

As book design is an integral part of the reading experience, we would like to acknowledge the work of those who shaped the form in which the story is housed.

Tessa van der Waals (Netherlands) is responsible for the cover design, cover typography and art direction of all World Editions books. She works in the internationally renowned tradition of Dutch Design. Her bright and powerful visual aesthetic maintains a harmony between image and typography and captures the unique atmosphere of each book. She works closely with internationally celebrated photographers, artists, and letter designers. Her work has frequently been awarded prizes for Best Dutch Book Design.

The picture of the seagull on the cover is called Close-Up Of Seagull Flying Against Sky and comes from the archives of Hollandse Hoogte.

The gull has been edited by lithographer Bert van der Horst of BFC Graphics (Netherlands) to make it appear to be flying out from the cover of the book towards the reader.

Suzan Beijer (Netherlands) is responsible for the typography and careful interior book design of all World Editions titles.

The text on the inside covers and the press quotes are set in Circular, designed by Laurenz Brunner (Switzerland) and published by Swiss type foundry Lineto.

All World Editions books are set in the typeface Dolly, specifically designed for book typography. Dolly creates a warm page image perfect for an enjoyable reading experience. This typeface is designed by Underware, a European collective formed by Bas Jacobs (Netherlands), Akiem Helmling (Germany), and Sami Kortemäki (Finland). Underware are also the creators of the World Editions logo, which meets the design requirement that 'a strong shape can always be drawn with a toe in the sand.'